A noise sounded downstairs.

Elena moved to the door and listened. She knew someone was down in the supposedly empty store. She turned off the light and reached for the phone, dialing 9-1-1. When the operator answered, she whispered her situation.

Pocketing the phone, she slipped out of the office and walked to the top of the stairs to listen. After a moment, she heard something move. She slipped back into the office and dug for Daniel's phone number. He answered on the second ring.

"Daniel, there's someone in the store."

"Elena?"

"Hurry." She heard someone walking up the treads and hung up. Where could she hide? The office had a large window with a fire escape. She hurried there, hoping she could beat the intruder. The old window hadn't been opened in years. She unlatched the window and pulled. It sounded as if the gates of a dungeon were opening, but it was her only hope.

LEANN HARRIS

Leann has always had stories running around inside her head. When her youngest child started elementary school, she finally gathered her nerve and began writing. She joined RWA in 1987 and is a charter member of Dallas Area Romance Authors and former president. Her first published novel was a finalist in the Romance Writers of America Golden Heart contest and was nominated by *Romantic Times BOOKreviews* as one of the best first novels in 1993. The author of eleven novels, her latest book is her first for Steeple Hill. She has a BS in speech from the University of Texas at Austin and is a certified teacher of the deaf, teaching deaf high school students algebra and chemistry. She's been married for thirty-five years and has two grown children.

Leann Harris
HIDDEN DECEPTION

Steeple
Hill®

Published by Steeple Hill Books™

STEEPLE HILL BOOKS

Steeple
Hill®

ISBN-13: 978-0-373-44302-4
ISBN-10:   0-373-44302-1

HIDDEN DECEPTION

www.SteepleHill.com

Printed in U.S.A.

The Lord is good, a refuge in times of trouble.
He cares for those who trust in him.
—*Nahum* 1:7

I'd like to thank:

My sweet husband, who cooked a lot of dinners.

My mom who always encouraged me.

And Sharon Mignerey,
who is the best "what if" partner.

ONE

Something was wrong.

Elena Segura Jackson stared at the open back door of her family's antique shop.

"Hello." Her voice echoed in the empty room. A shiver ran up her spine. "Joyce, are you here?" This was Joyce's night to lock up. Elena listened for a moment more. Nothing.

"Don't be silly," she chided herself. "You're acting like a five-year-old."

Shaking off her apprehension, she moved inside. *Where was the inside security light?* Reaching for the switch, she flicked it on. Nothing happened.

Her stomach sank. Taking a deep breath, she called out again, "Joyce."

The outside light did little to penetrate the vast darkness of the store. It was like walking into a cave, wondering what she'd find with her next step. She bumped into several pieces of furniture. Slowly, she made her way from piece to piece moving toward the stairs in the center of the room. The papers she needed were upstairs in her office. Halfway across the room, she stumbled and caught herself on the back of a chair.

"Wha—" She looked down. Her eyes followed a pair of legs up to a skirt and a blouse. The body lay against the large Spanish chest.

Slowly she approached the body. "Joyce?"

Kneeling, she shook her shoulder. "Joyce? Are you okay?"

Nothing.

Elena turned the woman over. It was Joyce. Her eyes were open, staring into nothing. Elena shook Joyce's shoulders, but there was no reaction.

Releasing her, Elena's fingers skated over Joyce's chest and encountered a wet spot. Elena jerked her hands back. Although she couldn't see the color of the liquid, she could smell the coppery scent. Blood.

Stumbling to her feet, she turned. A figure materialized out of the darkness, and before she could react, something crashed into her head turning the world black.

* * *

Detective Daniel Stillwater and his partner, Raul Rodriguez, climbed out of their police-issued sedan. Two police cruisers and the evidence van dotted the area around Amarillo Plaza in old town Santa Fe, closing down traffic on the street.

"Hey, Stillwater, you get this case?" Patrolman Mark Sanchez called out.

"We did. You the first responder?"

"Yeah, Icenhour and I caught the call. He's inside with the lady who found the body. She's not in too good a shape, crying and blubbering, but you know what a talker Icenhour is. He can soothe things over."

Daniel stepped into the antique shop and looked around. The overhead lights beat down harshly on the old furniture and elegant collections in the room. He couldn't figure out what folks saw in this old stuff. It looked like some of the stuff in his aunt's house. The evidence lieutenant looked up from his evidence kit.

"Find anything?" Raul asked.

"No." The tech stood. "There was a collection of smudged prints on the doorknob, but there's nothing I've discovered in the shop. The vic was stabbed several times in the chest and bled out."

"Thanks, Greg," Daniel replied. He scanned

the shop and didn't see anyone else. A set of wooden stairs divided the room, leading to the second floor. "Where's the witness?"

"She and Icenhour are upstairs in the office."

Daniel and Raul climbed the stairs, their shoes echoing heavily on the worn wooden treads.

"Is there anyone I can call for you?" Icenhour's voice floated out the open door at the top.

When they reached the top riser, they scanned the area. To the right, the space opened out to a storage area piled with boxes, chairs and carpets. To the left was a door marked Office. Looking inside, Daniel saw Icenhour sitting in a chair next to a woman. She held an ice pack to her left temple. In her late twenties, she had shoulder-length straight black hair with a sprinkling of bangs across her forehead. Those bangs brought a man's gaze to her golden-brown eyes. Twin tracks of tears ran down her pale, smooth cheeks.

She looked up, and Icenhour turned.

"Detectives, this is Elena Jackson, who found the body." He finished the introductions then stood. "I'll go downstairs and see if they need any help."

Raul took Icenhour's seat. Daniel grabbed a chair in the corner and pulled it close. He took a notebook and pen from his coat pocket. "Tell me what happened this evening, Ms. Jackson."

She set the ice pack on the desk. "I forgot some papers I needed and was coming back to the shop." She looked from him to Raul. "I found the back door to the shop unlocked, which alarmed me. Joyce is—was always so reliable about store procedures. But—"

Daniel waited for her to continue. He knew when to push a witness and when to back off and let them proceed at their own speed.

She wrapped her arms around her waist.

"But…" Raul prompted after several seconds.

Daniel threw him a look and Raul shrugged as if to say "someone had to."

"Joyce seemed to be distracted lately. I should've been more diligent and asked her what was wrong."

"So you think something odd was going on in her life? Did she have any family issues?" Daniel asked.

"I don't know. I think Joyce might have been divorced. She never talked about her past and wasn't looking for another relationship."

"Why do you say that?" Daniel asked.

"I've seen a couple of customers try to flirt with her. She shut them down. Politely, but she discouraged men. This last week, though, she was remote, as if something was bothering her."

"Have any idea what?" Rodriguez pressed.

She shook her head. "No."

Daniel's gut reaction told him the woman was hiding something.

"Did you have any cash on hand? Maybe someone was after money?" Daniel asked.

She shook her head. "I make the deposit run in the late afternoon. We don't keep a lot of money in the store."

"Is anything missing?" Raul questioned.

"Where is she?" A woman's voice floated up the stairs.

"Ma'am, you can't go up there," Icenhour replied.

"You want to try and stop me?" The steel in her voice caught both Daniel's and Raul's attention.

For the first time, Elena smiled. That smile tugged at Daniel's heart.

"That's Mom. You might as well let her up. She won't stop until she makes it up here."

They didn't need a scene. Daniel stood and walked to the door. "Icenhour, let the woman come up here."

Instantly, a woman appeared in the doorway and brushed by Daniel. In her early sixties, with blond hair and deep-blue eyes that burned with concern, she was a handsome woman, who bore no physical resemblance to her daughter. Instantly, she scooped Elena into her arms.

"Are you all right?" She pulled back and brushed Elena's hair from her face.

When Elena tried to speak, she couldn't say a word, but nodded.

"What have you done to my daughter?" the older woman demanded, turning to the detectives and glaring.

Daniel understood her reaction, but her attitude wasn't helpful. "Your daughter's—"

"Mom, the detectives have done nothing. Seeing Joyce's…body…reminds me of—"

The older woman nodded. "I want to take my daughter home."

Daniel glanced at Rodriguez, who nodded. "That's fine." Daniel reached inside his sports jacket, pulled out a business card and handed it to Elena. "If you remember anything else, please get in touch with me."

She took the business card and clutched it in her hand.

As the women started to leave, Elena paused and handed Daniel her keys. "Will you lock up?"

"Yes."

Once they were alone, Rodriguez stood and shook his head. "Talk about a mother bear protecting her young. I wouldn't want to get between that woman and her daughter."

Daniel slipped the keys in his pocket, then joined Rodriguez at the door.

"I know. Let's see if the guys downstairs have finished up."

He watched from the shadows as the police swarmed over the building. He ground his teeth. The stupid female showed up too soon. He hadn't finished his search. Of course, Joyce had surprised him, too. Threatened him, but he solved that problem. He could solve this new problem. There was another night, and he wasn't going to stop until he found what Joyce had stolen from him. Too much depended on that evidence, and he would find it.

When Elena walked into the Santa Fe police headquarters, the large clock on the wall read 6:20 a.m. It hadn't been a peaceful night. She'd wrestled "the nightmare," only this time it had a new twist. This time the dream started with her arriving at the antique shop and finding the body. But when she turned the body over, it wasn't Joyce she discovered. It was her birth mother's body, and suddenly the room had altered to the kitchen where her mother died. Her father, in a drunken rage, had grabbed a knife from the kitchen counter and stabbed her mother when she refused to get him another beer. Elena had been eight when that happened. Her older brother had called the police and held their mother while they waited for the cops.

It had taken years for that vision not to haunt her dreams. Too many times her adoptive parents held her while she cried. This morning she didn't want to add to the sorrow and grief her mother felt for Joyce.

After experiencing that old nightmare, Elena knew she couldn't go back to sleep, so she dressed and decided to go to work. Unfortunately, her car and keys to the shop were still with the detectives. Instead of waking her mother and facing questions, Elena wrote a note and took a bus downtown. She could walk from the main police station to the shop.

The receptionist walked to her desk, a cup of coffee in her hand. "May I help you?"

"Is Detective Stillwater here?"

The woman called the detective's extension. "Detective, there's a woman here—" She paused and looked at Elena.

"Elena Jackson."

The woman repeated the name. "Okay. I'll relay the message." She hung up the phone. "He'll be here in a moment."

Elena turned and looked out the plate-glass windows into the empty street. It glowed with a soft predawn light. The scent of piñon and mountain cedar filled the air. This time of day always refreshed Elena, and in the stillness, she could pray. She could tell the Lord about her day and spend time with Him. Even in New York, where there was a mass of humanity, the mornings were her time to renew herself. In New York, praying as she walked to work had made her appreciate the beauty of the city, but when she came home to New Mexico, her soul found peace.

The smell of the receptionist's coffee floated through the air, reminding Elena that she hadn't had her morning cup yet. A stop at Juan's at the corner of the street would be her first priority after she got her keys. Juan's Café was a favorite hangout for the cops and lawyers downtown, but, despite that, she'd wanted coffee and one of the breakfast burritos Juan cooked up. Often, when she was a teen, her adoptive father had brought her to the store and they'd stop at Juan's for a treat.

"How are you doing this morning?" Daniel's voice jerked her out of her thoughts.

Elena turned and watched the detective walk toward her. He was a good-looking man, something she hadn't noticed last night. Of course, she had been a little too preoccupied to look, but now she gave him a once-over. Whipcord lean, Daniel had a wealth of blue-black hair, high cheekbones, piercing brown eyes and a well-defined mouth. The coppery tone of his skin reminded Elena that it was his ancestors who first roamed this land. He probably had his fair share of female admiration. She didn't notice a wedding ring on his left hand. Although he'd been up all night, he didn't look tired.

"I came by for my keys. I wanted to get to the shop and see what needed to be done."

"Let's go back to my desk. Your keys are there and we can go over your story again."

Her eyes widened. "Why?"

"Now that you've had the night to think about what happened, maybe something else occurred to you."

Suspicion filled her. Did he think she had something to do with Joyce's murder? But before she could say anything, her stomach rumbled. Her cheeks burned with embarrassment.

Daniel's mouth curved with amusement.

"I haven't had breakfast," she mumbled. "I was going to stop by Juan's before I went to the store."

"Sounds good to me."

Her brows knitted into a frown. "I beg your pardon?"

"Let's go to Juan's. Over some burritos, we can go over your statement."

"Huh—" Her stomach rumbled again.

His gaze captured hers.

"Okay," she agreed.

Daniel went back to his desk, picked up her keys and handed them to her. He put his notebook in his shirt pocket, grabbed his corduroy jacket and slipped it on.

Rodriguez sat back in his chair. "Hey, when you're at Juan's, buy me a number one and have him send it over." He pulled several bills from his wallet and handed them to Daniel.

Elena noticed the silent message the two men exchanged and wondered what it was about. Once outside in the morning air, Elena glanced at Daniel.

"Am I about to get the third degree?" she asked.

"No. What makes you think that?"

"All the silent messages you and your partner exchanged."

"You're imagining things."

She didn't believe him and prepared herself for the grilling.

The wonderful smell of coffee and refried beans surrounded her as they stepped into the restaurant, making her worries disappear. Whatever the detective had in mind, she could handle it after a cup of coffee and something to eat.

She ordered and found a booth in the corner away from the noise and chatter of the restaurant. Daniel ordered his breakfast and Rodriguez's. After paying for them, he joined her.

"Have you remembered anything else about Joyce that you didn't tell me last night?" he asked.

"I've tried not to think, to put everything out of my mind." She concentrated on her burrito.

He took a bite of his breakfast. "How long did Joyce work at your store?" he questioned.

"She worked for my parents for the last five years." When he gave her a look, she explained, "I was in college at UNM, studying art. When I came home one Christmas, Joyce was working at the store. I knew her casually, but if you want more information on her, talk to my mother. Mom worked with Joyce every day for the last five years. I worked holidays and some summers when I came home. Once in New York, I rarely saw Joyce."

"But you've been here in Santa Fe for the last six months?"

Elena frowned at him. If he knew the answer, why ask the question? Maybe he was testing her. "My father passed away at the beginning of March. Mother wasn't able to handle the business, so I quit my job in New York and came home." She didn't want to discuss the grief that put her mother in bed or how in order to keep things running, she'd come home. Her adopted older brother lived in Seattle with his family. Of the two of them, she was more able to come and help their mother.

He took out his notebook and scribbled something down. "So you aren't familiar with Joyce?"

She frowned at him. "No. She was a wonderful employee, always on time, reliable, helpful to my parents. Since I've been home, I can't name any problems with her." Of course, Elena had been worried about Joyce.

"What are you not telling me?"

Her head jerked up. "What makes you think—"

He gave her a pointed stare. "I'm a trained investigator."

Elena shrugged. "As I told you last night, Joyce seemed to be preoccupied over the last couple of weeks."

"Tell me about it."

Elena tried to come up with exact instances. "One time she put the special orders in the wastepaper basket. Another time, she forgot to put a large check in the cash register. And another time, she came to work without her purse. She had to drive home and get it. That wasn't like her. When I asked her what was wrong, she told me she just had an off day. It wasn't an off day, but an off week. But I didn't press her. We all screw up."

As he jotted notes in a small spiral, the clatter of silverware and dishes filled the air. Elena tried to peek at what he wrote, but his head came up, and she smiled and settled back into her seat.

"And you never knew anything about her personal life?" he pressed.

Something was going on here. "No, I didn't, but I've got a feeling that you know something I don't."

He leaned back against his chair. "Did you know that Joyce had a criminal record?"

TWO

She looked stunned. "No."

"Hey, Stillwater." Jeff Muller, a patrolman and fellow soccer dad, walked up to the table. He nodded toward Elena. "You going to the girls' soccer game this afternoon?"

His daughter, April, and Jeff's daughter, Melissa, played on the same soccer team, the Red Peppers. They were 9-1 for the season. This was their final game. "I wouldn't miss it, Jeff. Has your daughter's injury healed?"

"Yeah. She's only got a few scabs left, but she's ready to play."

"I'll see you at the field at five."

Jeff nodded and walked off.

When Daniel looked back at Elena, he saw her struggling with the information he'd just dropped about Joyce. She was either a good actress or the info came as a total shock. His heart wanted to believe it was surprise, but his brain argued she could be acting.

Of course, he was fighting an unseen enemy—attraction.

She was the first woman who'd grabbed his attention since his wife's death. He'd found himself looking forward to seeing her today. Of course his reaction could be a combination of tiredness and hunger.

Liar, a voice in his head whispered.

"Are you sure you have the right woman?" she carefully asked.

They'd taken the dead woman's prints and run them through their AFIS computer system. Joyce Murphy's name and mug shot had popped up. "I'm sure. She'd been convicted of passing counterfeit money."

Elena's mouth fell open.

"So my news comes as a big surprise," he continued.

That jerked her out of her fog.

"Of course." She shook her head. "I never knew. She was a trusted employee. I'm sure my parents didn't know about her past. She was the only employee my parents had over the past few years, with the exception of my brother, Adrian, and me. Joyce was there for my mom when Dad had his heart attack and has helped since his death."

Elena's impression of Joyce didn't sound as though she continued her criminal ways. "Did your parents ever mention a concern about Joyce?"

"They never said anything to me. You could call my brother in Seattle to see if they mentioned anything to him. Of course, he left home before I did."

Elena's phone rang. She dug around in her purse and grabbed it. "Hi, Mom. No, I'm with Detective Stillwater." She looked up at him. "Did you know that Joyce had a criminal record?"

He watched her face as she listened to the answer.

"You did, but I don't—" Her hand curled into a fist. "Okay. No, I'll be at the shop in a few minutes." She closed her phone and carefully placed it in her purse. Raising her chin, she met his gaze. "Mom knew about Joyce's past. Are we finished? I need to meet her."

"We are for now."

"What does that mean?"

"I might have more questions as the investigation goes along."

She nodded, gathered her purse, and left. He carefully observed her. He'd checked out her background. Elena Segura Jackson had no criminal record. Adopted at the age of ten by the Jacksons after the trauma of seeing her mother murdered by her father, she'd had a normal life with teenage rebellion. She had one ticket for speeding, but that was it. Her college records showed her as an A student and her move to New York had been uneventful as far as law enforcement was concerned. He needed to interview the mother and brother. It might turn up something.

There was something that bothered him. It was this attraction thing. What he needed to do was to chalk it up to too little sleep.

His cell rang.

"Hey, Dad, are you going to be home before I leave for school?" April asked.

"I'm on my way, now, sweetie."

"Good. Grandma wants you to bring home some milk. She says you won't mind."

He laughed. His mother's friend, Rosalyn Mendoza, had come to his rescue when he came home from his unit in Afghanistan to take care of his wife, who had breast cancer, and daughter. His own mother had died before his daughter was born, but Rosalyn had adopted his daughter as if she were her own granddaughter. April only knew Rosalyn as her grandma. "You tell her I'll bring the milk. If she's plays her cards just right, I might bring home some apricot empanadas from Juan's." He knew the baked turnover was a favorite of his daughter's.

April cheered. "Hurry home."

He laughed. "You just want the empanadas before you go to school."

"No, Dad, it's you I want to see."

Her words brought on bittersweet pain that reminded him of how little he'd given his daughter over the years. But with the Lord's help, that would change.

Getting off the bus at the northwest corner of Amarillo Plaza, Elena tried to put aside the fear gnawing at her. She didn't want to think about what happened last night, but it seemed to race after her like a stalker. Hurrying past Mama Rosa's Cantina on the corner, Elena walked toward Past Treasures on the north side of the central plaza in old town Santa Fe. This square was part of the original city, built with adobe. Wooden beams used to construct the adobe stores were used to support the new wooden awning built to give shoppers shade in the middle of a blistering day. In the center of the square, old hitching posts were left to emphasize the history of the area.

When she got to the shop, there was nothing there to indicate a murder had occurred within those walls. All the police tape was down, but the door remained locked. She found the keys in her purse and opened the door.

With her hand on the knob, she prayed, "Lord, give me strength." Slowly, she entered the building. Her gaze scanned the room. The police had moved things, and there was black powder on several pieces of furniture and the back door.

Walking into the room, she heard voices coming from the janitor's closet at the back of the store.

"You don't have to do that yourself, Diane. Call your experts that deal with rugs."

From the voice, Elena recognized Preston Jones, the owner of the art gallery next door. Preston dealt exclusively with artists from Santa Fe, Taos and the surrounding area.

"Is there anything we can do for you?" Cam McGinnis asked. Cam owned the native jewelry store on the other side of the shop.

The three of them emerged onto the showroom floor. Cam carried a bucket, and Preston had sponges. Diane saw Elena, handed her rag to Cam and raced to her daughter's side.

"Oh, baby, how are you?" Immediately she was surrounded by her mother's favorite perfume. "I was so worried about you. How did you get down to the police station?"

"The bus."

Preston and Cam appeared behind her mother.

"How are you doing?" Cam asked, coming to her side. In his early fifties, he was a hippie, who came to Santa Fe in the early seventies and never left. He still bore some of his rebellious attitude toward the establishment and wore what was left of his hair pulled back in a ponytail. His salt-and-pepper beard was neatly trimmed. His designs had become famous, and he'd developed a wide following. He was also a major dealer of native jewelry created by local artisans.

Wrapping his arms around her shoulders, he hugged her.

She stiffened. "I'm okay." She didn't sound convincing to her own ears. When he released her, she stepped back.

Preston caught her gaze. "Are you sure?" He was the polar opposite of Cam. Preston Jones was tall, with a hundred-dollar haircut and clothes of the Hollywood elite, silk shirts and designer pants.

She didn't believe for a moment that he would help scrub this room. He'd probably give the sponge to her mother or Cam and then supervise.

"I can't believe what happened here." Cam looked around the room. "When I arrived this morning, the last of the cops were driving off. No one would tell me anything until your mom got here." Shaking his head, he asked, "Why would anyone want to harm Joyce?"

Elena looked at her mother. They needed to talk.

"Guys, Mom and I need a few minutes," Elena informed them.

The men glanced at Diane and she nodded.

Cam rested his hand on Elena's arm. "If there's anything that I can do, you let me know."

She appreciated Cam. He'd been a rock when her father died. Those first few days after she arrived home from New York City had been hectic, but if something needed to be done, Cam had stepped up and helped until Adrian had arrived from Seattle.

Preston nodded. "Those are my sentiments, too. If you need anything, call."

After the men left, Diane turned back to her daughter. "How are you?"

Elena sat down in the old rocker they'd recently

acquired. "I couldn't sleep, so I thought I'd go get my keys and purse from the cops. Detective Stillwater was still there."

Diane sat on the coffee table next to the rocker. "And—"

"Why didn't you ever tell me about Joyce's police record?"

Diane looked down at her hands. "It wasn't my secret."

"You didn't think I needed to know?"

"At the time, no." When Diane looked up again, she grabbed Elena's hand. "Do you remember when your father worked in the prison ministry?"

"Vaguely."

"It was something he had a passion for. He met Joyce while she was still incarcerated for helping her ex-husband to pass counterfeit twenties. Apparently her ex-husband convinced her to pass some of the funny money."

"She knew that money wasn't real?"

"Yes. When Joyce came up for probation, your dad was contacted and asked if he would sponsor her."

"So he agreed?"

"Yes. He believed Joyce had turned her life around and wanted to give her a new start. Your father trusted her. His trust was rewarded. Besides, your father's faith in her led her back to church."

Elena wasn't surprised by the news. Phillip Jackson had been a mighty man of God with a heart that encompassed all around him. He'd been a tall man, with a full head of black hair. His laugh had been a thing of pure joy, and his smile had eased her heart more than once. When the Jacksons had first adopted her, she remembered how nervous she was around Phillip, worried that his temper would flare out of control. That had been her experience with her birth father. He would rage, shout and strike out. If he was mad, everyone in the family knew to hide.

Elena remembered the first time she'd disobeyed Phillip. She'd been in the antique store and spilled her purple grape soda on her father's desk. She knew the rule about not bringing drinks into the office. When Phillip had discovered it, he'd been livid. He'd yelled and approached her. She covered her head with her hands expecting a blow. When nothing happened, she peeked through her fingers. Her father's stricken expression shocked her. He squatted before her and waited.

It took several minutes, but she lowered her hands. He then said the most amazing thing. "I'm sorry, Elena." She hadn't believed her ears.

"I was wrong to yell at you. Please forgive me."

Elena wasn't sure she heard right. "Huh?"

"I shouldn't have yelled. I'm sorry. Will you forgive me?"

It was the first time in her life anyone had asked for her forgiveness. But he didn't move and continued to look at her.

"Yes. I forgive you."

He nodded. "I give you my word, Elena, that I will never raise my hand to you. That doesn't mean that when you do wrong you won't be punished. But you will never have to fear me."

Her father had been true to his word. He'd loved her and guided her through her teens. She knew her father would forgive her, but there were consequences for doing wrong. Slowly over the years, she learned to trust, and God had worked through Phillip to show her what a true father would do for his child.

Phillip had been that way with all the people around him. "Why didn't you tell me about Joyce?"

"It happened while you were away at school. Besides, your father felt if Joyce wanted to share her past with you, she would've."

Oddly, the information made Elena feel worse. Why hadn't her father trusted her with that information?

"I guess I better start on the carpet." Diane stood and walked back to the spot where Joyce's body had been.

Elena came to her side. "I agree with the guys. Let a professional clean it."

After a moment's pause, Diane nodded her head. "Okay."

"I'll go call our regular guy." She started toward the office.

"Elena—"

She stopped and looked over her shoulder.

"It wasn't you, sweetheart. Your father thought it wasn't his secret to tell."

"I understand." But in her heart, she didn't.

When Daniel woke at two in the afternoon, he showered, dressed, and made himself a cup of coffee. The night shift always took it out of him or maybe he was getting too old for night shifts. On the refrigerator under the magnet from Carlsbad Caverns was the playoff schedule for April's soccer team. The final game was tonight at five. Her gym bag with her soccer uniform and shoes sat by the back door. He grabbed his digital camera, wanting to catch all the action of the game, and added it to the pile he needed to put into the trunk of his car.

Sitting down at the kitchen table, he opened his Bible to Ephesians 6 and read the chapter. Verse 11 jumped out at him—*Put on the full armor of God so that you can take your stand against the devil's schemes.*

He knew from experience how important that armor was. When he was in Afghanistan fighting with his unit, he felt at peace in the midst of the flying bullets and tank fire. But when the chaplain had told Daniel his wife was dying of cancer, he'd felt naked. He'd come home within days and had two weeks with Nita before she died. In those dark hours beside her bed, he realized what he'd done to his wife. He had more of a bond with the guys in his unit than his wife. She hadn't blamed or accused him of being a rotten husband, but she exacted a promise that he would not leave April. It was a promise that he'd not broken.

Shaking off the memories, he closed his Bible, snagged April's gym bag and walked to his car. "Thank You, Lord, for another chance with April."

He loved every moment with his little girl.

Walking into the police headquarters, Daniel met Raul. He held up the file in his hand. "ME's preliminary report."

The news stunned Daniel. "Already?"

"Amazingly, there was a lull at the morgue, so he got to our vic. She was stabbed four times. With the first three, our perp missed her heart. It was the final blow, straight into the heart that killed her."

Obviously the crime had occurred at Past Treasures. Had the murderer been trying to rob the shop, or did it have something to do with Joyce's life? "You want to interview the surrounding shop owners to see what they know?" They needed to know more about the victim. The square where the murder had occurred had a very low robbery and murder rate.

"I do. Let me get my coat and we'll canvass the area."

Once Raul got his coat, it took less than five minutes to get to Past Treasures. The store remained closed and Daniel didn't see activity inside. They walked next door to the art gallery.

A tall, distinguished-looking man with a full head of dark hair and a deep tan approached them. "Gentlemen, how may I help you? Are you here to see the latest Jean-Paul Jaunes painting before it flies out the door?"

"I'm Detective Daniel Stillwater and this is my partner, Detective Raul Rodriguez. We're with the Santa Fe Police and are investigating the murder of Joyce Murphy."

He shook his head. "When I saw that Diane hadn't opened the store, I went over there to see what the matter was. That was so tragic."

Raul scowled. The guy was putting it on rather thick.

"Could we speak to you about Joyce?" Daniel asked.

"Of course. Why don't we talk in my office?"

They followed him to the back of the store. His office was off the back workroom. Paintings, storage crates and bubble wrap filled the room, but no one was in sight. Mr. Jones walked to the enclosed office in the front corner. He'd spared no expense in furnishing the room, from the antique Spanish desk to the Tiffany lamp on the desktop. Beside it sat a laptop, open and working. Motioning to the chairs before the desk, he sat in the chair behind it.

Once settled, Daniel asked, "How well did you know Joyce?"

"She worked next door for several years. We traded hellos, but I didn't know her very well."

"Did you ever see her with a boyfriend? Or a friend she hung with?"

"No. The woman was completely closed up. She didn't do small talk."

Raul leaned forward. "Did she ever come over

here and look at your gallery? Maybe talk about business at the store next door?"

"She came over here a couple of times. She didn't appreciate fine art. And she couldn't afford it. I told her it was a good investment, but she didn't believe me."

Daniel jotted down a couple of notes. "Do you know if anyone had anything against Joyce? Someone who she had a fight with."

"I can't say I ever saw anyone fight with her. But she mentioned working at the homeless shelter, the food bank and her church. There are plenty of people at the homeless shelter you can't trust. Try there."

"What church?" Raul asked.

"First Community Church over on St. Mary's Avenue."

"Did she ever mention anything about her past?" Daniel wondered if Joyce had told anyone about her time in prison.

"Nothing. One time I asked about her plans over the Fourth of July holidays—if any of her family was coming into town. She said nothing about family and planned to stay in town."

"Can you think of anything else about Joyce? Habits, likes, dislikes?" Daniel hoped that Preston might help provide a clue to Joyce's killer.

"She loved the Dodgers. Knew all the members of the team. She was something of a baseball fanatic."

That piece of news could help. "Did she like college baseball?"

"Can't say. You might ask Diane or Susan and Jeff Marks over at Mama Rosa's."

Daniel glanced at his partner, silently asking if he had any questions. Raul shook his head.

Pulling out his business card, Daniel handed it to Preston. "If you think of anything else, call me."

Preston dropped the card onto his desk. "Sure."

The detectives started out of the store, but Raul stopped by a large painting of a lily on a branch. Daniel had to swallow his smile at his partner's puzzled expression.

"Are you interested in buying a good piece of art?" Preston flashed a smile at the detectives. "I have several up-and-coming local artists. You can buy them at a reasonable price before they become famous."

Raul's eyes widened. "There's a market for this stuff?"

Jones bristled. "This is the Jean-Paul Jaunes painting I told you about earlier. He is the hottest upcoming painter on the art scene in the Southwest."

Daniel grinned. Raul was more into the bold colors of his conquistador ancestors.

"Well, for that price, he better be number one."

The painting's price was equal to two months of a detective's salary.

"It is an investment, Detective."

"Yeah, well, I'd rather put that kind of money in a good car," Raul replied.

Preston sniffed and walked away.

"Apparently, you have no taste," Daniel teased.

"No, I just have common sense. I don't plan on being robbed." Raul nodded to the door.

They walked down the street to Cam's jewelry store, Three Star Creations, located on the south side of Past Treasures. The instant they walked into the store, Cam looked up from the customer he was helping. "I'll be with you gentlemen in a moment," he said, and went back to helping his customer. While Cam finished up, Daniel surveyed the store. Three Star Creations had a name in the city for its unique and inventive pieces.

When the customer finished her purchase and left the store, the man turned to Raul. "What can I do for you?"

Daniel stepped forward and introduced himself and the other detective. "You know about the murder of Joyce Murphy."

He shook his head. "I couldn't believe what I saw when I came to work this morning. I've been sitting with Diane and Elena all morning."

"Can you tell me anyone who might want to hurt the victim?"

"No one. Of course, I wasn't close to Joyce. She kept to herself. Wasn't very friendly."

"Did she ever mention anything about her past?" Daniel wondered if Joyce had told anyone about her time in prison.

"Nothing."

"Is there any incident that you can think of where Joyce had a run-in with someone? Or maybe she mentioned someone who was angry with her."

"No."

"No boyfriends?"

"She never mentioned anything to me, and I never saw anyone."

Daniel handed him his business card. "If you think of anything else, please give us a call."

He nodded.

As they walked to the next store, Daniel muttered, "So far all we know is the woman was perfect."

"And that bothers me," Raul answered.

It was a red flag for Daniel, too.

* * *

Daniel and Raul walked the length of the alley behind the shops on the square. Cars from the shop owners and their employees dotted the alley. Parked behind the back door of Past Treasures was a cleaning truck. Daniel walked up the three steps that led to the door. The top step broadened out to make a small landing.

Carefully, he studied the back lock.

"Do you think it was a random robbery?" Raul asked. He glanced up and down the alley.

"Could be, but why not break into the jewelry store or the art gallery? Wouldn't it be easier to fence jewels or one of the smaller paintings than some antique chest?"

"Naw, you couldn't give away that art, but you might be able to get rid of the jewelry."

Daniel studied the back door. "I don't see any signs of the lock being forced."

Raul joined Daniel on the top step. "So a pro did this, not an amateur or some teenager high on something."

"Sounds right to me. Let's check the statistics on robberies in the area, but I don't think it was random. I think whoever broke in was after something in that shop."

The back door opened and a man stepped out

with a steam cleaner. He looked up and stopped. "The store's closed today."

"I was so sorry to hear about Joyce." A woman's voice floated out of the open back door.

Daniel pulled out his ID and showed it to the man. He shrugged and walked to his truck.

"Is there anything I can do for you?" the woman continued.

"No, but thank you. There's nothing at the moment."

Daniel recognized Elena's voice.

He knocked on the back door to announce their presence.

Elena and her mother and another woman turned toward the sound.

"Detective." Diane Jackson moved forward. "Is something wrong? Do you need more information?" A hint of panic colored her voice.

He smiled to ease her anxiety. "We've come to look at your shop in the light, to see maybe where the murderer might've come from."

All three women paled.

Daniel turned to the woman he didn't know and introduced himself. "And you are?"

"Susan Marks. My husband and I own Mama Rosa's on the corner of the square."

"Did you know Joyce?"

"Yes, I did. She helped with the homeless shelter. We donated food to the facility, and she helped us take it over there and serve."

"How long has she been doing that?" Raul questioned.

"The last year and a half."

"Have you noticed anything unusual about her in the last few weeks?"

"No." Susan glanced at her watch. "I need to get back for the dinner rush."

Daniel pulled out his business card and gave it to the woman.

After she left by the back door, he turned to Elena and her mother. "I'd call a locksmith today and have that back lock switched out. Whoever broke in here didn't have a difficult time. Make it harder for anyone if it happens a next time."

THREE

Elena opened the door to Joyce's house. The modest dwelling on the edge of a business district had originally belonged to Phillip Jackson, but he'd sold it to Joyce for the mighty sum of fifteen hundred dollars. That information her mother told her after her father's funeral had amazed Elena, but as she thought about it, it made perfect sense. Her father was an exceptional man.

Pausing inside the door, Elena let her eyes adjust to the darkness of the room. The room looked as if a bomb had gone off in the place. Sofa cushions were pulled off and split open. In the corner, the desk had been ransacked, drawers hung awry, papers scattered about.

The kitchen mirrored the living room, with drawers hanging askew and dumped on the floor. Walking down the hall, she peeked into the bathroom. Same song, second verse. In the upstairs bedroom, the bed had been dismantled, the mattress pulled off the bed. The dresser drawers were thrown about the room with the mirror ripped off, the shattered remnants scattered over the top. Numbly, she walked around the room and glanced into the closet. Oddly enough, nothing was disturbed.

Elena pulled her cell phone from her purse and dialed 911 as she walked toward the bedroom door. Suddenly, a figure appeared in the doorway.

Without thinking, she used her purse as a weapon and aimed at the man's head. She made contact. He stumbled back into the hall and she tried to race by him. He lunged for her and caught her around the waist. Their momentum carried them to the floor. Somehow, he twisted in midair and took the brunt of the blow when they landed. She was ready to fight for her life when she looked into the man's face and saw Daniel Stillwater. She went limp.

He said nothing.

In the quiet, she heard the 911 operator calling.

"Ma'am, are you okay?"

Scrambling away from Daniel, she yelled. "What's the matter with you?"

He slowly got to his feet and offered his hand. "Are you all right?"

She took it and stood. "No."

"Ma'am," the operator called.

She could chew him out later, but now she needed to tell the operator she was okay. She looked around in the hallway for the phone.

"Ma'am," the operator again called.

"Where is it?" Elena said, frantically scanning the hall. She stepped back into the bedroom. There between the mattress and a drawer lay her phone. Snatching it up, she said, "Uh—I'm sorry."

"Are you all right?" the operator asked.

"Yes, but—"

"Are you being held against your will?" the woman questioned.

Color filled Elena's face. "No, no. It's just that I thought the intruder was—"

Daniel motioned for her to give him the phone. She did. He quickly explained the situation to the 911 operator, gave his police ID number and told her to notify the units on the way that he was with Ms. Jackson. He also asked for an evidence team to be dispatched to this address. He disconnected and handed the phone back to Elena. "Let's go and greet the officers."

She dropped the phone into her purse and followed him to the door. Outrage and mortification had replaced fear in her brain. "You nearly gave me a heart attack. You're lucky I didn't use the move my father taught me when he knew I was going to New York City."

His brow arched. "You're lucky I didn't shoot you as an intruder."

That gave her pause.

"What are you doing here?" He was all business.

"The medical examiner released Joyce's body. I told Mom I'd get something for the funeral home to dress Joyce in." She looked into the bedroom. "But someone had decided to destroy the place before I got here."

"So it was this way when you entered?"

She frowned at him. "Yes, it was. Do you think I did this?"

He said nothing.

"I got here about five minutes ago. I was so stunned that I couldn't believe my eyes. I had just decided to call 911 when you appeared in the doorway and we did that little thing." Her cheeks heated with embarrassment.

His lips twitched.

When they arrived at the front door, the patrol units were already there.

Reaching for the doorknob, Daniel said, "I'll have to commend patrol division on their quick response time."

Elena frowned. That wasn't exactly her first thought.

He called out to the patrolmen, then slowly appeared in the open door. The patrolmen holstered their weapons and walked to the front door. Elena recognized them. They were the same ones who responded to Joyce's murder.

"Stillwater." Icenhour nodded to the house. "What are you doing here?"

"Our murder vic from yesterday, this is her house. I wanted to let you know that Ms. Jackson and I were inside and the robbery call-in was a misunderstanding. No use having you shoot me."

Icenhour nodded. "It would be hard to explain how I shot a Santa Fe Police Detective."

Daniel pointed over his shoulder. "Someone has systematically destroyed the house. I want to see if we can get usable fingerprints. Also, I want you to look around the property and see what you come up with."

The two patrolmen nodded and walked away. Daniel turned to Elena. "Do you still want to get a dress for Joyce?"

Tears welled up in her eyes, but she refused to cry. "Yes."

He nodded and indicated for her to go back inside. "Why is your family handling the burial?

Why doesn't Joyce's family take care of those arrangements?"

"Her parents disowned her and wanted nothing to do with her after her time in prison. Apparently, she never mentioned them again."

He studied her, then nodded. "Follow me." They walked into the house, up the stairs to the bedroom. He stepped into the closet. "Pick out something."

Crowding into the closet by him, she tried to focus on a dress. Suddenly, the grief, fear and uncertainty swamped her. She didn't want to cry. She wouldn't cry. All the clothes blurred, and tears ran down her cheeks. The harder she tried not to cry, the more she did.

"Are you all right?" he softly asked, his lips close to her ear.

She couldn't speak, so she nodded.

When he touched her shoulder, the dam broke and the tears flowed unchecked. Unseeing, she turned into his chest. All the turbulent emotions she'd bottled up poured out of her.

She didn't know how long she bawled. A minute or eternity, but when the storm had passed, she stepped back. On his shirt was a big, wet spot.

She motioned to the spot. "I'm sorry."

His eyes held a wealth of understanding and the gentle smile curving his lips eased her embarrassment. "Don't worry about it. At least you didn't throw up on me as my daughter has after a crying spell." He handed her his handkerchief.

She laughed in spite of herself. "At least there's that."

Noise from the outer room startled them.

Daniel stepped out of the closet and said something to the patrolman. She used the time to gather her wits and dry her face.

When he came back, he said, "The patrolmen found the back door open. Our perpetrator came in that way."

She nodded and then turned her attention to picking out a dress. She grabbed a soft blue one with a matching belt and a wide lace collar, pulled it out and showed it to Daniel.

"Let's take it downstairs where I can note what you took and then you can deliver it to the funeral home."

It was quickly done, the garment's pockets checked for anything. When nothing was found, he allowed her to leave. As she drove away, fear clutched her heart. Just what had Joyce been involved in that someone would search and trash her home with such violence?

But that wasn't the only worry slithering

around her brain. She didn't know what it was, but it was there. "Lord, help. Give me Your guidance and protection."

He watched from his car as she drove away. The cops quickly left the scene after her. His fingers wrapped around the steering wheel as anger shot through him. This was the second time she barged into the place he was searching. The woman was becoming a complication he couldn't afford. Joyce had uncovered the truth and threatened him with it. He wanted that proof destroyed.

He would find it, no matter what it took. He wouldn't go to prison. Not again.

Daniel finished taking down the last license plate from the cars parked on the road beside the grave, then slipped the small spiral notebook into the inside pocket of his sport jacket. He'd run checks on cars and their owners when he got back to the office, then compare notes with what his partner turned up. Hopefully, Raul had tracked down Joyce's family.

He walked over the sand and stones to the grave site and joined the mourners. There were only a handful of people. Elena and her mother, Preston Jones, Cam McGinnis, Carolyn Ellis from the homeless shelter, and Susan and Jeff Marks, owners of Mama Rose's Cantina.

"Lord," the minister began, "accept the spirit of our sister and comfort those who grieve for her, we pray. Amen."

Each person held a rose and as they filed by the coffin, they put a rose on the closed lid. When Elena looked up, she stopped.

"Detective Stillwater."

Before he could respond, Cam McGinnis moved behind Elena. His expression and the set of his body signaled the coming flare-up.

"What are you doing here?" he demanded.

The words exploded in the silence of the overcast morning.

Everyone froze.

The color left Elena's face. "Cam, let me introduce you to the detective who is working on Joyce's murder."

Cam's expression hardened. "I know who he is. He and the other detective visited my store yesterday. There's no reason for them to be here at the cemetery." He pointed at Daniel. "He's spying on us, aren't you?"

The man's reaction told Daniel that Cam had experienced some run-ins with the police before now. He wondered what the man was hiding. "I'm here to pay my respects to Ms. Murphy."

Cam snorted but before he could say anything else, Preston grabbed his arm. "Quit making a fool of yourself, McGinnis. This isn't the seventies."

He glared at Preston. "I know that."

Diane Jackson linked her arm with Cam's. "Why don't you drive me back to the shop?"

The lady smoothed over the tense situation, winning Daniel's admiration.

The guests walked to their cars.

Once they were alone, Elena said, "I'm sorry about Cam. I don't know what's gotten into him." She shook her head. "Joyce's murder has put us all off our stride. Cam is usually so mellow. What are you doing here?" she asked.

"I wanted to see who attended the funeral. It's not unusual for a murderer to attend his victim's burial."

Her brown eyes darkened with fear.

"Did you know all the people who came to the cemetery?"

"Yes."

"Have you thought of anyone who had something against Joyce?" Daniel asked.

"No. Joyce worked, went to church, helped at

the homeless shelter. Nothing that would make anyone angry enough to kill her."

There were a lot of upstanding people who had secret lives. "If you think of anything, call me. You still have my card?"

"Yes. Did your daughter win her soccer game?"

Of all the things she could've asked him, never would he have thought she'd ask about April's game. Her concern told him about her heart.

"They won, 7-6."

Again he saw her smile. It lit her face with a glow that drew him. "Tell your daughter congratulations."

As he watched her drive off, he noticed a figure behind a large stone cross two hundred yards away. The instant the man saw Daniel, he quickly disappeared among the other headstones. By the time Daniel could run to the headstone, the man would be gone.

As he walked back to his car, Daniel knew his hunch had been right. Someone here had information he needed.

Sitting across the desk from Raul, Daniel ran the last of the license plates he had taken down that morning. They were the only detectives in the large room that housed the homicide division at the moment. Most of the other detectives were at the birthday party for the head of homicide.

"You see anything unusual at the graveside service?" Raul asked as he read over the primary autopsy report, again.

"No. A few of the local merchants showed up."

"No friends or male acquaintances?"

Sitting back in his chair, he looked at his friend. "No."

Raul eyes widened. "And how long had the lady lived in Santa Fe?"

"Let's see." Daniel looked at his notes. "It's been five years since Joyce finished her prison sentence."

"I did locate a brother of hers." He looked at his notes. "Bozeman, Montana. He said their parents were dead, and he didn't have any use for a sister who threw her life away."

Raul had done the background check on their victim. Daniel shook his head. The brother's callous attitude wasn't that unusual. Sad, but not uncommon.

"None of her friends showed up at the funeral besides the folks you saw?" Raul frowned. "That seems mighty strange to me."

"My thoughts exactly. What has the lady been doing in the intervening years?" Apparently, they needed to talk to a few more people. "What about that ex-husband of hers?"

Raul looked into the paper file. "Bryce Green." He typed the name into the criminal database. "Ah, our boy was released from prison two months ago. His parole officer is in Albuquerque." He glanced at Daniel. "I'll give him a call."

Daniel's computer screen beeped, letting him know the last license plate came back. Apparently, the little sports car belonged to Preston Jones. There was no one there at the grave site that shouldn't have been, except the far-off witness. But did any of the shopkeepers have records?

He typed Jones's name into the AFIS system to see if the man had ever been printed. He also entered Cam McGinnis. He wanted to know why Cam had a chip on his shoulder.

"So he's never checked in?" Raul replied into the phone. He explained about Joyce's death. "Thanks for the help."

"Got anything?" Daniel asked.

"The ex never checked in with his parole officer. He's going to put out a warrant. What did you turn up?"

"Two hits—Jones and McGinnis. Jones has a conviction of stalking his girlfriend. The incident had happened nearly twenty years ago. Cam had been arrested for possession of marijuana."

Raul shook his head. "Let me guess. Some sit-in that happened in the sixties or seventies."

Daniel nodded. "You nailed it. It was 1975 here in Santa Fe. They were protesting against the destruction of trees around Taos. He was convicted and paid a fine. But since that time both men have been picture-perfect."

"Do you believe that?" Raul asked.

"Let's say my skepticism is strong."

"Detective Stillwater, here is the lab report on the break-in." The young officer handed the folder to Daniel.

Opening it, he scanned the results. "The door was jimmied, but the prints on the knob were smudged. There was nothing we could use." That was not unusual. "Only type O blood had been found on the carpet. The vic was type O."

"Yup." Raul ran his hands over his face. "So what we got is a big zero."

"No, what we have is someone looking for something as evidenced by the scene at the victim's house. I wish I could've ID'd the man I saw at the cemetery." That bothered him.

They had another player in this little drama, and

he didn't know how that player was connected. They were uncovering more suspects by the minute.

Elena helped Susan Marks wheel the large pan of enchiladas into the Blue Mesa Homeless shelter. Every Thursday, Joyce had helped Susan deliver food to the shelter, then volunteered her time. Elena knew that Susan didn't have the time to stay and help Carolyn Ellis with serving the meal, so she'd volunteered to help.

Knowing in her heart that helping Susan was the right thing, Elena still had to pray for the strength to take Joyce's place.

"I can smell those enchiladas across the room," Carolyn said as she moved to help with the rolling cart. "And I'd say the dining room is always more crowded the days you bring food."

Susan grinned. "It's good to know."

"Did you bring any flan tonight?" one of the men in the main dining room asked.

"Sorry, not tonight. But I did bring some pan dulce."

"That will do. Those sweet breads are the best I've tasted."

They wheeled the pan to the serving table and quickly unloaded the enchiladas and Spanish rice.

"I've got to get back," Susan announced. "My night manager is sick tonight." She rushed out.

Carolyn smiled at Elena. "Thanks for helping."

Elena nodded, but before they could exchange any other words, people started down the dinner line. A man, one she'd never met before, stepped behind the table to help serve.

The man, in his midforties with brown hair and green eyes, and a killer smile pulled an apron from the cabinet beneath the table and tied it around his middle. Turning, he nodded to Elena. "I'm Frank Gleason. I'm the new volunteer here." He held out his hand.

"Elena Jackson. Are you—"

"Hey, I'd like some of those enchiladas," one of the homeless men said.

"We can talk later."

It was forty-five minutes later when the last man came through the line. Nothing remained of the dinner.

"Does this always happen?" Elena asked.

"It does on the nights Susan and Jeff bring the food," Carolyn answered.

Frank smiled. "And the crowd's always bigger on those days."

"Do you work here every night?" Elena asked.

"No. Just Tuesdays and Thursdays."

"And, of course, it couldn't be because of the food, could it, Frank?"

He grinned. "I did save a little pan dulce for myself."

Elena laughed. "I wasn't as wise, but I might stop by Mama Rosa's and have something to eat."

"If you are going there, would you take back the pans for me?" Carolyn asked.

"Sure."

It took only ten minutes for Carolyn, Frank and her to clean the pans and load them into her car.

"After smelling all those enchiladas, I might visit Mama Rose's myself," he said.

"I'd welcome the company," Elena said.

Smiling, he nodded. "I'll meet you there."

It seemed ridiculous for her to drive the half block, but the metal pans were awkward. It took less than a minute to make the trip. She struggled to maneuver the pans out of the backseat, but managed finally. When she tried to close the door while balancing the pans, one started to slip. She tried to catch it, but the pan went one way and she another. Strong hands caught both the pans and her arm.

"Thank you," she said and looked up, expecting to see the face of Frank. Instead it was Detective Daniel Stillwater.

FOUR

"What are you doing here?" The question popped out of her mouth before she could think.

His brow arched. "I'm taking my daughter, April, out to dinner."

Elena looked over his shoulder and saw a young girl, probably eight or nine, with long black hair and chocolate-colored eyes. She watched Elena intensely.

"Oh." Mortified, Elena smiled at the girl.

"Do you work at the restaurant?" April asked.

"No. I work in my family's antique shop around the corner."

"And they sell pans?" the young girl asked.

Elena smiled. "No. The owners here help feed people at the Blue Mesa Homeless Shelter. I'm bringing the pans back. I also thought I'd eat some of those wonderful enchiladas after smelling them for the last hour."

"Come and eat with us," April replied.

The idea of eating with the detective and his daughter was both appealing and weird. She looked around and saw Frank. "I was going to have dinner with Mr. Gleason."

He stopped beside the group. Elena introduced the two men.

Frank smiled. "Much to my embarrassment, I forgot I have a previous engagement." His gaze met Elena's. "Maybe we could postpone our dinner?"

"Of course."

He nodded and walked back to the Blue Mesa. Elena's face flamed.

Daniel took the pans from her. "Our invitation is still open."

"It'll be fun," April added. After a moment of Elena's indecision, she added, "Please."

Elena glanced at Daniel. He gave his daughter a stern look. "I will not forget about the meeting with your teacher," he warned.

She hung her head.

He turned to Elena. "Please join us. I'm sure April would enjoy the company."

April's head came up and she smiled.

"I'd be happy to, but first let me give these pans to Susan."

Daniel nodded toward the front door. "Lead the way."

The moment they entered the restaurant, Susan saw them. She hurried to the entrance.

"Let me take those." She waved to one of the waiters and they took the pans from Daniel.

"The enchiladas smelled so good that I needed to come and have some. None were left at Blue Mesa."

"My grandmother will be delighted with the news. We use all of her recipes here at the restaurant. Come, I'll show you to a table."

Once they were seated and had placed their orders, April asked, "How do you know Papa?"

Elena glanced at Daniel, wondering how he wanted her to answer that question.

"I am helping Elena with a problem she had," Daniel offered.

"What kind of problem?"

Before Elena could answer, the waiter brought corn chips and drinks.

Elena didn't want the young girl to know about Joyce, so she diverted her by asking, "What grade are you in?"

"I'm in the third grade," she proudly announced.

"And do you like going to school?" Elena asked.

"Usually." She looked down at the table.

Elena glanced at Daniel. She saw his eyes dancing with merriment.

Elena waited, knowing there was more to the story. "What happened today to make you not like school?"

April looked down at the table. "I kicked a boy."

She raised her head and spoke to Elena. "The boy said my dad was one of those cops who put the wrong person in prison. He said Dad didn't know anything, that he was only a stupid cop. I kicked him."

Elena's gaze locked with Daniel's. She fought back a smile, but she saw Daniel's pride shining in his eyes.

"When I was in school, the third grade," Elena whispered, leaning close to April, "there was a bully who always made fun of me. One day he cornered me on the playground, calling me names." The boy had made fun of her father's drunken behavior the day before. "He got in my face and I punched him."

Daniel and April looked at her. "I got in trouble, big time, but that boy didn't ever mess with me again."

"Really?" April asked.

"Yes, but later I learned the boy's father beat

him. His heart was hurting. What I should've done was ask the teacher for help. I also should've prayed for him. Did you think that maybe someone in the boy's family that you kicked might have someone in jail? It's easier to blame others for our faults."

April frowned. "That's what Dad said."

"Your dad knows what he's talking about."

She raised her head. "Yeah, I know." Father and daughter exchanged smiles.

Their dinner arrived. As they ate, Elena saw Daniel's pride in his daughter. It reminded her of her adoptive father's pride in her. It also told her about the detective. He loved his daughter.

And that touched her heart in a way she couldn't explain.

Daniel sat on the bed next to his daughter. She had her favorite stuffed animal, a fuzzy white rabbit that her mother had given to her on her third birthday. After Nita had died, that stuffed rabbit had helped April feel close to her mother.

They prayed and he kissed her good-night. As he was leaving, April said, "I like her, Dad."

"What?"

"I like Elena. She's pretty and she talked to me like I was a person, not just a dumb kid."

He didn't know what to say. "I agree. She's a nice lady."

"I hope I get to see her again."

"Go to sleep, April. And no more kicking the boys."

She giggled.

He moved down the hall to the spare bedroom that he used as a library. In the hall hung a picture of Nita and him at their wedding. They'd been high-school sweethearts. They married the day after they'd graduated. After six months of his working on the dock of a local shipping company, Nita discovered she was pregnant. He knew they needed more money for the baby so he'd joined the army. And found his calling. He'd done one tour of duty and came home. Nita hated the army, but Daniel loved it. He didn't re-up but joined the Santa Fe PD. He also signed up for the National Guard.

When his Guard unit had been called up, secretly he'd been delighted. And that guilt rode him hard. He discovered that he had more in common with his team members than his wife. He wouldn't make that mistake again. April would have a full-time father, who was here for her. He couldn't undo his past, but he'd made peace with Nita before she'd died.

Walking into the library, he thought about Elena Jackson. He wondered if the story she told April was true or just her kind heart wanting to put a child at ease. Sitting at his computer, he pulled up the case file. He wanted to know more about this woman who touched his daughter's heart.

Daniel walked into Santa Fe police headquarters at nine-fifteen the next morning. He'd run late because he'd stopped by the school and walked April to her class. It wasn't hard to identify the young man she'd kicked. He glared at her from across the room. Several of the kids greeted April as a conquering hero.

Miss Baxton announced that both April and Tomás would be staying after school for the next week to clean up the room. Neither April nor Tomás was happy with the result, but that was the principal's ruling.

Daniel moved to where Raul sat behind his desk, studying his computer screen. He looked up. "The boss has been here wanting to know what we've gotten on the Joyce Murphy case. I told him there were no suspects thus far. The lady appeared squeaky clean. He wasn't happy."

"We can canvass more of the shops in the square to see if anyone knew Joyce."

Daniel sat on the corner of his partner's desk. "Okay, we've got no good leads. What if we go back to the square and put the word out that we're looking for information on the case. Let everyone know any tips we get will be eligible for a reward?"

"Sounds good to me. Anything to generate a lead."

They headed for Amarillo Square. The Blue Mesa Homeless Shelter was around the corner from the square. They parked in the side lot and walked in the main door. Daniel looked around for Carolyn Ellis, the shelter's director. They found her in her office.

"What can I do for you, gentlemen?" Carolyn asked.

"Tell us about Joyce," Daniel replied.

She sat for a moment, thinking. "You know, it's strange that I can't tell you anything about the woman other than to tell you she worked here on Tuesday and Thursday nights."

"Did she tell you about herself?" Raul asked.

Carolyn closed her eyes and sat for a moment. "No, I can't say she told me anything about herself. We talked about the shelter, what needed to be done, how we could get the money, but now that I think about it, she told me nothing of her past."

Daniel leaned forward. "Did she tell you anything of a personal nature? What she liked or didn't like?"

"No, but she told me she admired Mr. Jackson. That he was a hero in her eyes."

"Did you wonder about that?" Daniel pressed.

"No. Everyone knew what a good man he was. He helped in his church, worked with a prison ministry. If you needed something, you could count on Phillip. When I needed someone to work a shift here, I could call him and either he or his wife would show. We all admired him. When he died of that heart attack—" She shook her head. "We all miss him. I know that Diane was relieved when Elena came home. I'd never seen Diane that crippled before. She couldn't function at all after Phillip died. Elena coming home saved her."

Daniel pulled a business card out of his shirt pocket and handed it to Carolyn. As they were leaving the office, Daniel turned back to her. "Who's the new person working here at the shelter? He was here last night?"

"That's Frank Gleason."

"What does he do?" Daniel asked.

"He told me he works in the banking industry. He's here in Santa Fe to do some training with First National of Santa Fe. His family's in

Colorado, and he wanted to do more with his evenings than sit at a hotel. He's been a blessing."

"Would you have a phone number for him?"

"Not current. I had a number that I called when there was a change in the time for him to work. The desk clerk said he wasn't registered. When I asked him about it, he said he'd moved hotels and didn't know the number of the new place. He promised to bring it to me. I just never got the name of the new hotel or number. But he's always been faithful to show up the night he's supposed to work."

"Did he know Joyce?" Raul asked.

"I can't say. They worked together a couple of times."

"Was there any problem?" Daniel followed up.

"No. But now that I think about it, that first night that he was here, Joyce left very early. When they worked together, she was all business. I think he wanted more, but she'd have none of it."

"Thanks for the information."

As Daniel and Raul walked to their car, Raul asked, "Why are you concerned with this Frank Gleason?"

Daniel stopped by the passenger side door. "Because there's something about the man that sets my teeth on edge."

"You think he's not what he claims to be?" Raul answered.

"When he was introduced to me yesterday evening, he changed his plans to have dinner with Elena very quickly. And he wasn't smooth with the excuse."

Raul's eyes widened. "You had dinner with Elena Jackson last night?"

Daniel pulled open the car door and got in. Raul slid behind the driver's wheel and started the engine. "Well," he prompted when Daniel remained quiet.

"I took April out to dinner last night after our conference with her teacher." Raul knew that Daniel had been called away from work to deal with his daughter's offense. "I decided April needed a boost after being dressed down. We met Elena outside Mama Rosa's. That's when this clown thought he could hit on her."

Raul looked at his partner and wisely didn't say anything. The words that had just spilled out of his mouth surprised Daniel as much at they surprised Raul. It was a cardinal rule of police work that you didn't get involved with the suspect or victim in any investigation.

"Anyone else we haven't interviewed?" Raul asked.

Daniel pulled his notebook out of his shirt

pocket. "Let's see. Our last ones are Susan and Jeff Marks, the owners of Mama Rosa's."

Raul revved the engine and headed around the square to where the restaurant was located.

Elena tried to focus on the computer screen as she entered the last of the figures for the day's receipts for the bank deposit. Their business had been brisk that day. She couldn't say if curiosity seekers had come to the shop to see where the murder had happened or their new merchandise, bought from the Riva's old homestead, but the shop had been crowded with people all day. Oddly enough, they'd had the best day of sales in the last year. Cam teased her that perhaps they should have a murder more often. His receipts for the day had also hit record numbers. She'd glared at him. What was the matter with the man? He'd gone ballistic with Daniel, acting as if he'd committed the murder, yet here he was teasing about it.

She'd tried not to think about the detective today but failed miserably. What had caught her attention was how he dealt with his daughter. It appeared she was a handful, but that handful was all energy and intelligence. Elena hadn't meant to share her story of punching a classmate who mentioned her father's drinking, but Elena knew the hurt and confusion April felt. Phillip had shown her how to handle vicious talkers. It had been such a wonderful comfort to Elena that she'd wanted to share it with April. The verse in 2 Corinthians 1:4, *...so that we can comfort those in any trouble with the comfort we ourselves have received from God,* popped into her head.

Elena understood April's pain. And although their situations were completely different, their pain was the same.

Just as Elena hit the print button, she heard something downstairs. She moved to the door and listened. She heard nothing, but knew someone was in the store. She turned off the light and reached for her phone, dialing 911. When the operator answered, she whispered her situation.

Pocketing the phone, she slipped out of the office and walked to the top of the stairs to listen. After a moment, she heard something move. She slipped back into the office and dug for Daniel's phone number. She called it. He answered on the second ring.

"Stillwater."

"Daniel, there's someone in the store."

"Elena?"

"Hurry." She heard someone walking up the

treads and hung up. Where could she hide? The office had a large window and a fire escape outside that window. She hurried there, hoping she could beat the intruder. The old window hadn't been opened in years. She unlatched the window and pulled. It made the most dreadful noise, as if the gates of a dungeon were opening.

"Lord, help," she whispered.

Daniel had been on the way home when he got Elena's call. His heart jerked in his chest and he had to fight the alarm and remain calm. He contacted dispatch.

"We've already sent units, Detective."

He prayed while he ran every red light. Turning into the square where the shop was located, he saw no PD units. He stopped in front of the shop, and raced out of his car. Drawing his weapon, he tried the front door. It was locked.

He raced down the sidewalk to the end of the shops and ran into the alley. The back door of the shop hung open. Above the back door, on the balcony, Elena squatted, hunched into a little ball. He moved beside the door.

"Elena," he whispered.

Her head came up and her gaze locked with his.

He pointed to her and silently asked if she was

okay. She nodded. He motioned to the building, asking if the intruder was inside.

She shrugged her shoulders.

He debated whether to wait for backup or just charge into the building. The decision was taken from him when he heard the patrol cars. One pulled into the alley. The officers raced out and joined him. Together, they cleared the bottom floor. It took another eight minutes to clear the second floor.

He holstered his gun and walked to the window. "Elena, it's all clear," he called out before he stuck his head out the window. She stood, a metal candlestick in her hand.

He held up his hands. "My weapon's holstered."

Her shoulders sagged. Moving to the window, she handed him her weapon, then stepped inside. Her foot caught on the windowsill and she tumbled into his arms. When he caught her, she wrapped her arms around his neck and buried her face in his neck.

His heart jerked, relieved she was okay. He tightened his hold on her, thanking the Lord she wasn't hurt. He couldn't say how long they stayed locked in each other's arms, but one of the patrolmen called out "all clear."

"Detective?"

The patrolman appeared in the doorway. He saw them, and Daniel nodded him off. His eyebrow arched, but he holstered his gun and walked off.

Elena's grip lightened.

"Are you all right?" he whispered.

The death-grip stranglehold she had on him loosened. "Yes."

"Were you hurt?"

Her face flamed with color. "No." Her arms dropped to her sides and she stepped back.

"Everything okay in here, Detective?" the other patrolman asked.

"The lady's a little unsteady right now. Give me a second and I'll talk to you." He turned back to Elena. "Why don't you sit down and I'll see what the patrolmen have uncovered."

She nodded her head, but refused to look at him. He didn't know if she was still afraid or embarrassed by her actions.

As he walked out of the room, he didn't know what to think, either, but he did offer the good Lord thanks.

FIVE

Elena took several deep breaths, trying to still her galloping heart. She'd been ready to jump off the balcony when she heard Daniel's voice.

"Thank you, Lord," she whispered. She'd never been so glad to see a person as she had when he put his face out the window.

She should be embarrassed about nearly strangling him, but she couldn't dig up the shame.

"Everything secured downstairs. Apparently, your burglar got in the back door again. You didn't put on the new lock as I told you to do."

She looked up at him from the chair she'd collapsed into. "It will happen tomorrow, first thing."

He nodded.

"Do you think it was the same person who killed Joyce?" she whispered.

His hesitation was all she needed to know. "We can't be sure."

She stood, wrapping her arms around her waist. "He's after something here, but what?"

"You don't know that for sure."

She straightened her shoulders and glared at him. "Has Cam's store been broken into? Or Preston's shop? No, I'm the only one. Now why is that?"

"Okay, if we go on that assumption, what is it you have in here that is so unusual or different that someone would break in here?"

"We sell antiques. Most of what we sell are large pieces that are not easily moved. At Christie's, where I used to work, we got a lot of jewelry and things that could easily fit into a burglar's pocket. We have very few things like that here."

"Walk downstairs with me and let's look around."

She nodded. "All right."

Together they walked down the steps. The patrol officers were gone and the back door locked.

He surveyed the room. There were a few vases and paintings. "Can you think of anything that has excessive value?"

She pointed to a few pots made by Hopi Indians in the middle of the nineteenth century.

"These would bring a high price, but you'd have to know what you were looking for." She pointed to the woven baskets on a shelf. "Anasazi. Those baskets are also very expensive, but then again, you'd need to know what you were looking for."

"So probably your common junkie wouldn't have any idea the worth of those pieces?"

"True."

"Where do you keep the jewelry you sell?"

"I take it out of the case and put it in the safe upstairs."

He scanned the room.

"What are you looking for?"

"I'm trying to imagine what the thief was looking for, but I can't see it."

"Look around if you like. I need to finish the bank deposit."

He turned to her. "After your receipts?"

"Joyce didn't handle those. Either Mother or I did. Before Dad died, he was the one who made the bank run."

"I'll wait for you and see that you get safely out of here."

She wanted to tell him it wasn't necessary, but in her heart she felt gratitude he was willing to stay. "Thanks."

Leaving him to wander around the showroom floor, she raced up the stairs to finish the paperwork. It only took her ten minutes to finish entering the receipts and make up the bank deposit. Clutching the bank bag, she turned off the lights and walked downstairs. Daniel slowly walked around the display area.

"Have you come up with anything?" she asked.

"No. I'm blank. Obviously, my lack of experience in your field is showing."

"Well, I'm doing no better. I can't tell you what the thief is after. Now, that wardrobe over there is eighteenth-century Spanish, but it was built here in Santa Fe by craftsmen in the New World. But no thief is going to be able to cart if off. Or that side table."

They walked to the back door.

"Tomorrow, you are going to have new locks installed, yes?"

"Yes."

"And video cameras aren't a bad idea. You might catch a picture of who's breaking in."

"I'll talk it over with Mom."

He nodded. "I'll follow you to the bank." She opened her mouth to protest, but he held up his hand. "Humor me."

She nodded.

Once the store was locked, Elena walked to her

car. He followed her. She paused, and looked at the ground, unable to look him in the eye. "I'm sorry about choking you earlier."

When he didn't immediately respond, she looked up.

A beautiful smile curved his mouth. "It was understandable."

He wasn't going to embarrass her. "Thank you."

She started to get into the car, when he touched her arm. Stopping, she looked at him.

"Elena, I want to thank you for your words to April. I know it helped her. She's still working through her mother's death."

"I knew what she was feeling. I was a little older than she was when I lost my mother. And although the circumstances of her death were totally different, you hurt. My adoptive parents held me many a night when I had nightmares about her death. They made a difference. I wanted to try and help."

Their gazes locked. "My thanks," he murmured. So much was in his eyes beyond gratitude. "There's one more thing I want to ask you. Last night, the guy who joined you at Mama Rosa's, do you know him?"

"No. I've never seen him before yesterday. Carolyn told me he's been volunteering. Why?"

He shrugged. "He didn't seem too eager to stick around once he knew I was a cop. I wonder why?"

"Sorry, I can't help."

"You've answered my question."

How she did that, she didn't know, but she slid behind the wheel of her car and started toward the bank. Looking into the rearview mirror and seeing Daniel trail her made her feel as if God had given her a protector.

She wondered how Daniel would feel about that description.

Elena stifled a yawn. She and Cam sat in the little coffee shop across the square from their shops.

"Excuse me."

"Not sleeping well?" Cam observed.

"Yeah." She didn't sleep well again last night. She had another nightmare where Joyce's death mixed up with her mother's. Diane had found her in the kitchen with an empty plate sprinkled with crumbs of pie. Diane simply took her hands and prayed with her for God's peace. Elena had gone back to bed, but couldn't go back to sleep.

"That's understandable."

"Have you had any trouble with break-ins at your place?"

"No. But I take everything out of the cases and lock it in the safe. You think it was random?"

She rubbed her head. "I don't know." She ran her forefinger around the lip of her paper cup. "Do you mind if I ask you a question?"

"Of course not."

"Why were you so outraged at Detective Stillwater at the grave site?"

All expression left his face and he sat back in his chair. "I've had a few bad run-ins with cops."

She nodded, but his vagueness could've been anything from murder to a speeding ticket.

He looked at his watch. "I probably need to go. If you need any help, let me know." With those words, he shot out of the coffee shop.

Obviously, Cam had some bad experiences with the police and wasn't willing to talk about them. Leaving the shop, Frank Gleason waved to her.

"Good morning, Elena."

"Frank." He seemed to appear out of nowhere.

"Mind if I walk with you? I wanted to explain about dinner."

Her radar went on alert. "What about dinner?"

"I didn't want you to think I ditched you on purpose."

She continued to walk to her shop. "I didn't think that. Of course, the detective thought differently."

"What?" He reached out and stopped her with his hand.

Startled, she looked down at his hand resting on her arm.

Jerking his hand away, he said, "Sorry. What did he want to know?"

"Who you were and how long had I known you?"

"What did you tell him?"

Where had his concern come from? "The truth. I just met you."

"Oh."

"Is there a problem?"

He seemed to snap out of some sort of funk. "No. All I wanted to say was I did forget about a meeting I needed to have with some of the bankers I've been with this last week."

Suspicions swirled around her mind. "I didn't think anything about it."

"Okay. Are you going to work again at the shelter?"

"If Carolyn needs help, but I've got too much with the shop."

He paused for a moment, considering his answer. "I hope to see you soon."

She nodded and walked to her shop. She didn't notice it last night, but Frank acted like a man who had secrets, and he didn't want them revealed.

When she got to the door of her shop, she turned and noticed a stranger with a camera. He was taking pictures of her shop. She went inside and walked to the office upstairs. Moving to the window, she looked out into the street. The man had disappeared as quickly as he appeared.

She didn't like the feeling. Someone was spying on her.

Daniel hung up the phone after his conversation with Elena's brother, Adrian Jackson. He only knew the victim casually and had nothing more to add to what Elena had said about Joyce.

"What'd the brother say?" Raul asked.

Daniel filled his partner in on the conversation. He sat back in his chair. "What's wrong with this picture? Are we chasing after ghosts, or was the vic the prime target of this murder?" He rubbed his chin. "The lady's been a model citizen since she was released from prison. It seems her problems were connected to her ex."

"When I talked with his parole officer, I learned the man was released from Los Lunas last August." The Central New Mexico Correctional Prison was located in Los Lunas. "With him never showing up to check in with his parole officer, he's shot up to the top of my suspect list."

Daniel walked around his desk to see Raul's screen and stopped dead. The man in the mug shot was the man Elena was talking to last night. "He's here in Santa Fe, but passing himself off as Frank Gleason."

"How do you know?"

"I saw him last night. He's the guy working at the homeless shelter."

"The guy's working for Carolyn?"

"That I don't know, but he helped last night at the shelter. I know because when Elena introduced April and me, he made his excuses and ran."

"I'll give his PO a ring to see if I can get any more leads."

Daniel's cell rang. "Stillwater."

"Detective, this is Elena Jackson. There was a man in front of my shop, taking pictures."

There had to be more to the story. "Do you know him?

"No."

"Did he threaten you in any way?"

"No, he didn't speak to me in any way."

"What was it that alarmed you?"

"Well, I probably wouldn't have freaked, but he took several pictures of me as I walked across the square from the Coffee Cup. When I went inside our shop and looked back out the window, the man simply vanished. It made me nervous. Also, he was here yesterday taking pictures."

"I can be over there in a few minutes."

"No, you don't need to come." He could hear the embarrassment in her voice. "I just wanted to tell you about it."

"Don't be embarrassed. You did the right thing."

"Thanks."

He closed his cell. Turning to Raul, he said, "You know that feeling I told you about that things didn't seem right…it just was confirmed."

Elena helped her mother carry the last of the apples to the dunking booth. The Fall Carnival was an annual event that First Community Christian Church put on every year. Diane was in charge of entertainment for the kids. Diane had always had a way with children. She'd been the Sunday school teacher for the fifth grade, and she also always taught Vacation Bible school. Her mother's skill had also been a blessing when the Jacksons had adopted her. Elena had been shy and reserved, never wanting to call attention to herself, because if her birth father saw her, he was as likely to smack her as say good morning.

The big sheet-metal tub filled with water stood under the trees on the west side of the church.

Diane's cousin had volunteered to man the store today.

"Hello, Elena."

She spun around and looked into the face of April Stillwater. "How are you doing?"

"I'm fine." April smiled at Elena. "I wanted to thank you for telling me that story the other day. It helped."

Elena glanced at her mother and introduced the two.

"Would you like to be the first one to bob for an apple?" Diane asked.

"Sure."

April stepped up to the tub. "What do I do?"

"Try to catch an apple with only your mouth," Diane explained.

April threw her a questioning look.

"It can be done," Diane assured her. "Elena was the number one bobber in fifth, sixth and seventh grade."

April turned to her, questions in her eyes. "I'm not sure it can be done."

"You going to show her?" Diane asked.

"You know it's been a long time since I did this kind of thing," she told April.

"Yeah." Her doubt rang clear.

"Is that a challenge?"

April shrugged, but hope burned in the little girl's eyes.

"Okay." Elena looked around for something to tie back her hair. In the next booth, they had twine. She cut a piece and tied her hair back. Moving to the tub, she knelt. "Now, you have to hold your hands behind your back." She demonstrated. "And now, catch an apple."

The first time the apple escaped her. They all laughed. It took another three times for her to snag the apple. She pulled the apple from her mouth and said, "I was better a few years ago."

Diane threw her daughter a towel and Elena dried her face.

"Would you like to try?" Elena motioned toward the tub.

April grinned. "Looks like fun." Eagerly, she knelt, put her hands behind her and went for an apple. Her first try, the apple escaped. Try two, she dunked her face and came up laughing. On the third try, she snagged an apple. By this time, there were several other kids watching the fun.

"Who wants to be next?" Diane asked.

A boy around April's age stepped forward.

Elena handed the towel to April and they watched as the new volunteer tried for an apple. It took him six tries before he caught the apple.

Another boy took the first one's place.

"Is your dad here?" Elena asked April.

"He's in the tent behind the church. He's helping Grandma make fried bread."

The appealing scenario couldn't be ignored. "You mean he can cook?"

"Sort of. Grandma Rosalyn does most of the work. He just watches the bread and pulls the pieces out of the oil when they're done. You want to come see? Gran's fried bread is the best."

"I have a weakness for fried bread. Let's go."

Half a dozen tents dotted the parking lot of the church. Several of the women had set up booths and provided various goodies. There were also booths filled with crafts and some of the farmers had brought in vegetables and fruits. There was a table of face painting for the kids and sign-ups for volunteers to help families in the church with car repairs, handyman services and health screenings.

Under a big tent in the back corner, Daniel stood over a large pot of grease. To the side of him was a woman in her sixties. Her black hair streaked with gray was pulled back into a long braid. From the efficient way she worked the dough, it was obvious the woman knew her business.

"Dad, look who I found," April called as they neared the table.

Daniel looked up and smiled. Elena felt it all the way down to her toes. Her heart's reaction puzzled her. She didn't know this man in any other capacity but in his professional one.

"Did you fall in some water?" Daniel asked his daughter.

"No, I went bobbing for apples at Elena's mom's booth. You should try it. It was fun."

The vision of him trying to catch an apple brought a smile to Elena's face.

The woman kneading dough laughed. "I would like to see that."

Daniel glanced at the older woman. "You don't think I can do it?"

She laughed. "No. I don't think you can."

"I know a challenge when I hear it."

The older woman wiped off her hands. "I'll finish frying this bread while you show your daughter you can grab an apple."

Amazingly, he good-naturedly took up the dare. "But you won't be there to see me."

Her eyes gleamed with mischief. "Don't you worry, Daniel Stillwater. You go show April what you can do. I'll get someone to take over here."

He stepped aside, took off the apron and grabbed April's hand. "Show me the way."

The girl grinned at her father. "This way."

Elena watched in awe as this detective who was used to dealing with death took his daughter's hand to go bobbing for apples.

The duo stopped and glanced over their shoulders. "Aren't you coming?" Daniel asked.

It was an invitation she couldn't refuse.

SIX

Daniel grabbed the apple with his mouth and pulled it out of the tub of water in triumph. It had only taken fifteen tries and three dunkings, but he caught the apple. Hearing his daughter's laughter had driven him.

"Ha, Dad, it only took me three times to get the apple," April gleefully informed him.

Water dripped off his hair into his eyes. Removing the apple from his mouth, he shook his head like a dog. Elena laughed and handed him a towel. Standing, he wiped his face and hair. His shirt clung to his chest. He tried to dry it as well as he could.

"I look like a drowned rat."

"No, you look like a wet papa."

April's words went straight to his heart. They were golden, and he thanked the Lord for the laughter and joy in those words. His gaze met Elena's, and he saw the admiration in her eyes. And attraction.

"You do look like a wet man." Although Elena's words were simple, he read a wealth of meaning and respect in them.

Cam McGinnis walked up to the dunking booth. "What are you trying to do, Elena? Drown the cops?" His comment jerked everyone out of the teasing mood.

"We're seeing who can grab the apple in the least amount of time. Want to try?"

"I didn't bring a change of shirt. Besides, I don't want to leave my booth for long. I have Sarah covering for me while I get something to eat."

"Grandma has fried bread if you want to have some," April volunteered.

"Sounds good. Lead the way."

Daniel and Elena walked behind them. He took a bite of the apple he paid so dearly for.

"She's a charming girl," Elena commented, watching April.

He looked at April. He thought of his past mistakes and knew how April and Nita had suffered. He wasn't going to repeat the error. "She's my heart."

"Do I detect more in that statement?"

He took another bite. "No." He didn't want to talk about his failings. "Did you know that the man you worked with the other night at the shelter was Joyce's ex-husband?"

She stopped and stared at him. "Are you sure?"

"I'm sure. He's going by the name Frank Gleason here in Santa Fe, but his real name is Bryce Green. He served a twelve-year sentence for passing counterfeit money."

"How do you know?"

"Because when we ran a check on Joyce's ex-husband, his picture popped up on our computer screens. I recognized him." He started walking. He didn't want Cam to get too far in front of them especially since his daughter was with him.

Elena followed. "I wonder if he contacted Joyce?"

"Yes. They worked shifts at the Blue Mesa. If he approaches you again, call 911. He's not compliant with the terms of his parole."

She nodded.

When they arrived at their booth, Cam had bought several pieces of fried bread and already finished a piece. "Good," he mumbled.

Rosalyn laughed. "What happened to you, Daniel?"

"I finally got the apple, but it took a few tries."

Cam bought a drink from the next booth and walked back the way he came.

Daniel took the last bite of apple and tossed the core into the trash behind the booth. Slipping on the apron, he moved Rosalyn out of his way so he could watch the bread she had in the oil.

Elena stepped to Rosalyn's side and whispered something.

Rosalyn laughed.

He wondered what those two were up to. It worried him.

Elena felt silly pumping Rosalyn for information on Daniel, but something inside of her wanted to know more about the man.

"I'm April's honorary grandmother. Daniel's mother was my best friend. She died when Daniel was in high school. He has an older sister, but she was away at college. I didn't want that girl to come home to take care of her brother, so I became his guardian. But he's always been like a son to me.

"He married too young, but he and Nita were in love." She shook her head. "It didn't take long for reality to hit them. Money was scarce and when Nita became pregnant, Daniel joined the army. Nita wasn't happy." She fell silent. Glancing at Elena, she shook her head. "I'm a busybody. But I will say that Daniel Stillwater has always been an honorable man."

Elena felt like a Peeping Tom, wanting to look into this man's life, but she wanted to understand him. True, she didn't have to understand the cop looking into Joyce's murder, but she couldn't stop asking questions and wanting to know more about him. And his connection with his daughter told Elena about the kind of man he was.

The day passed with laughter, companionship and good food. They walked through the booths, observing the handiwork of numerous church members. April commented on most of the booths and knew the people running them.

April thoroughly charmed Elena. The little girl was a combination of inquisitiveness, intelligence and mischief. She would be a handful for any parent, but sometimes this strong detective seemed to be at a loss as to how to respond to some of her comments. But no matter what April said, Daniel listened and tried to keep up.

Leaning close, she whispered, "She's running over you."

Daniel smiled. "I know. And I scramble every

day trying to keep up with her. Little girls are a mystery."

His puzzlement made her laugh, bringing to life all sorts of feelings she hadn't expected.

Looking up, Elena spotted the man who'd been taking pictures of her the day before. The man had a camera in his hands. "Daniel, there he is. The man who was taking pictures of the store."

He immediately went into cop mode. "Stay here." He disappeared into the crowd.

"Where's Dad going?" April asked.

"To find someone for me."

A small frown gathered between April's eyes.

"Trust me. He'll be back."

"He promised me he wouldn't ever leave me again." She looked around at the booths packing up. "He's been to war, did you know that?"

"No. I didn't know that."

"Mom told me he was fighting for America in a faraway place. When Mom got sick, he came home." April looked up at Elena. "He didn't smile a lot when he came home. And he was very sad when Mom died. So was I." She crooked her finger and Elena leaned close. "I heard him laugh last week. I guess it's okay to smile again."

April's words stole Elena's breath. She squatted and looked into April's eyes. "I know your father will always miss your mother. I still miss my mom, but your mother and my mother wouldn't want their families to be sad forever. When I think of my mom, I smile and remember her smile and laugh. That's what I think your mom might want for you."

A tear ran down her cheek. "I'm glad 'cause sometimes I feel guilty if I want to laugh."

An arrow shot through her heart. "Don't. I know your father doesn't want you to be sad all the time."

April wrapped her arms around Elena's neck. She felt the little girl relax. "I'm so glad."

Daniel reappeared and stopped cold when he saw April and Elena. Elena met his questioning gaze. "Your papa's here," she whispered to April. The girl pulled back and looked over her shoulder.

Daniel knelt before his daughter. "Are you okay, sweetheart?"

She nodded and walked into her father's embrace. His eyes closed.

"She was a little concerned when you disappeared so quickly."

He ran his hand over April's head. "I'm not leaving, April."

She didn't say anything but lay her head on her father's shoulder. Standing, he held his daughter in his arms. When he started walking, Elena followed.

"I couldn't find the man. He disappeared before I could get to him."

"But you saw him?"

"I did."

They reached the booth that Diane Jackson ran. Elena stopped. "Thanks for a nice day, April, Detective."

"What was that about?" Diane asked.

"It was about a little girl who misses her mother."

Diane stepped forward and wrapped her arms around Elena. "I'm proud of you," she whispered.

The circle had been completed. *Comfort those with the comfort you've received....*

He watched from the side street, and saw the cop and Elena talking. The day they spent together made it look as if they were in love. So the detective was more interested in the woman than what happened. That worked for him. He still hadn't located where Joyce hid what was his. But he would find it. He couldn't afford not to.

Elena arrived at work with Diane.

"Good morning, ladies," Cam greeted them in the alley behind the shops.

They greeted him.

"How's things going on the investigation into Joyce's murder?" he asked.

"I'm not sure," Elena answered.

"You spent the day with the detective, yesterday," he commented.

Diane opened the back door and walked into the shop. Things were out of place. A couple of vases had been knocked over and fallen to the floor, shattered. The doors of several armoires stood open.

The three of them stopped.

"Not again," Diane commented.

Elena pulled the cell phone out of her purse along with Daniel's business card and called him. He answered on the second ring.

"There's been another break-in at the store," Elena told him.

"Don't touch anything. I'll be right there."

"What's going on here?" Preston's voice rang out. He stood at the back door.

"We've been hit again," Diane explained.

Preston joined them. "Why on earth is this happening?"

Diane sat down. "I wish I knew."

Elena moved around the room, checking to see what else was out of place. It appeared nothing had been taken, but several things had been knocked to the floor. "I'm going to check the office. Maybe someone was trying to get cash."

The office had received the same treatment that the furniture downstairs had gotten. Desk drawers hung out of the computer table. The filing cabinet had also been searched.

Preston joined her.

"Whoever did this was up here, too."

He walked around the room. "Could someone have been looking for money?"

"We don't leave cash in the store overnight. I know you don't, either."

He rubbed his chin. "This doesn't make sense."

She turned to him. "Nothing makes sense. What is going on, Preston?"

He pulled her into his arms. "I don't know. Maybe we should spend a few nights in the shop to make sure no one breaks in again."

She pulled back. "That's not a bad idea."

"See. Us artsy guys have good ideas."

Diane appeared at the doorway. "Oh, no."

Behind her, Cam peeked over her shoulder.

"Preston has a good idea. Maybe we should have someone stay at the store for the next few days."

A frown furrowed Diane's forehead. "What's in

the shop is not as important as someone's life. But I think maybe a good security firm might be the answer."

"Hello."

Cam and Diane walked down the steps. "Detective," her mother greeted Daniel.

She hurried out of the office and walked down the steps. Daniel moved around the showroom, taking in the mess. He looked at the back door. The old lock was still there.

"I called the locksmith," Elena explained. "He was supposed to come and replace the lock."

"I'd call a different one and make sure it happens today. I'll get the evidence guys out here to see if they can lift prints." Daniel turned to Cam and Preston. "We'll need your prints for elimination purposes."

Cam tightened up. "I don't know why you'd need mine. I didn't date Joyce. Preston did, but I didn't."

The room fell silent.

"I didn't know that you were seeing Joyce." Elena directed her statement to Preston.

He puffed up like a rooster and shot daggers at Cam. "I did not date that woman. She and I worked late several nights and decided to go to dinner. Friends sharing a meal. Nothing more, nothing less. If I recall—" he glared at Cam "—you weren't particularly fond of Joyce after she made a couple of comments on your jewelry and the prices you charged."

Daniel stepped in between the two men. "I don't think this is the place to air your complaints with each other. If you want to come down to the police station with me, you two can talk to me and my partner."

"Is that an order?" Cam snapped.

"No, it's simply a request. No one is under arrest, and I just want to explore your thoughts on what you just mentioned."

Cam looked down at the carpet. "I'm not interested in talking to you."

Preston nodded. "I'll see you ladies later." He strode out the back door. Cam followed him.

Elena stumbled over to a red leather-and-wood chair. "I never would've believed that Preston and Joyce dated."

Daniel pulled out his cell and called for the forensic team, then opened the notebook he carried in his jacket pocket and wrote something down. "Did either of you know about Preston and Joyce?"

"No," Elena replied.

Diane shook her head. "I never saw anything

between them. And if they ever went out to dinner with each other, I didn't know anything about it."

"But with what has happened over the last few months, Mom, it would be easy to overlook something like that."

Diane looked at her daughter. "You're right." She turned to Daniel. "With my husband's death, there were a lot of things that escaped my notice."

Leaning forward, Elena added, "I'm not much help, either. I spent months trying to get my footing here. Joyce covered a lot of nights for us."

A knock on the back door brought their attention to the back of the store. Two men with Crime Scene Tech printed on their shirts stood at the door.

Daniel motioned them inside. "Come in, guys. See if you can pick up any prints on the back door. And upstairs in the office."

The technicians nodded. One stayed at the back door, while the other man went to the office.

"Ladies, you'll have to stop by headquarters and be printed in order to eliminate your prints. It won't matter when you stop by. We have folks who can print you 24/7."

"I guess crime doesn't take nights and weekends off," Diane observed.

"True." He nodded to them and walked out the back door.

Diane looked around the showroom. "Looks like we've got to do some cleaning, again."

Daniel walked to the jewelry store to follow up on Cam's comments. He decided not to wait because he didn't want Cam to think up ways to cover his tracks.

Daniel knocked on the back door. It was still too early for the store to be open. Cam answered.

"Mr. McGinnis, I would like to follow up on your statement there at the Jacksons' store."

Cam didn't look too happy, but after a long pause, motioned Daniel inside.

"What do you want to know?" He stood by the safe at the back of the store.

"You mentioned that you thought Joyce and Preston dated. Why do you think that?"

He looked around the store, and then shrugged. He'd made some decision. "One night after I'd locked up my store and went out to my car, I saw Joyce get into Preston's car and they drove off together. That happened another couple of times. When I asked Preston if he and Joyce were an item, he didn't respond. I thought he was just being discreet."

"Did he ever mention her again?"

"No. And I thought the two of them were kind of an odd pair."

"Why would you think that?"

Shrugging, Cam said, "Preston goes for flashier women. And he likes to talk big. Joyce wasn't flashy, and she didn't strike me as someone who'd fall for the line Preston puts out."

Not knowing Preston well, Cam's assessment of his fellow store owner struck Daniel as true. "Anything else you can think of?"

"No."

Daniel offered his hand. Cam looked at it as if it were a snake. After several seconds, he took Daniel's hand and shook it.

"Thanks for the info, McGinnis. If anything else occurs to you, please call."

Daniel's next stop was the art gallery. Preston didn't answer his back door, so Daniel had to walk around the block and bang on the front door. A perturbed Preston marched out of his office. He opened the door. "What?"

"I'd like to ask you a few questions," Daniel calmly answered.

Preston took several deep breaths and brought himself under control. "I'm sorry, Detective. I'm ready to punch a bigmouthed jeweler."

"So what he said wasn't true?"

Preston jerked his head back. "Joyce and I went to dinner a couple of times, but McGinnis made it sound like we were more than casual friends. We were working late on the Fourth of July plans for the entire block. Since Diane and Elena were still concerned over Phillip's death, Joyce helped with some of the decisions we had to make. McGinnis doesn't know anything about it since he sat on his backside and let other people work. He's probably had dinner with Joyce as much as I. Check at Mama Rosa's. I think that Cam and Joyce used to have a standing lunch date on Thursday."

"All right. I'll check that out."

"Believe me, Detective, Joyce wasn't my kind of woman."

"Thank you, Mr. Jones." Daniel opened the door and paused. "Be sure to go and be printed today so we can eliminate your fingerprints from the crime scene."

A tight smile curved Preston's mouth. "I'll do that."

Daniel would be interested to see who showed up at police headquarters and got printed. He wondered if Cam McGinnis would voluntarily show up. Of course, it wouldn't matter since his prints were already on file.

As he walked out of the store, he saw Bryce

Green on the other side of the street, watching the art store. When Bryce saw him, he disappeared around the other side of the street.

That was one more suspect he needed to talk to.

SEVEN

"If you want to clean your hands, use the wet wipes behind the ink pad," the jailer instructed Elena. When she showed up at police headquarters, one of the jailers wasn't busy and took her fingerprints.

Elena pulled the moist towelette from the container and wiped the ink from her fingertips.

"We're finished here," the woman said. She took the fingerprint card and walked to her desk. Elena stepped out of the room and ran into Daniel.

"Whoa." His arms shot out and grabbed her shoulders, preventing her from falling.

"I should've watched where I was going."

"I'm glad you're here because I wanted to discuss something with you about Joyce's murder. Why don't we go to my desk where we can talk?"

She nodded and followed him down the hall.

The double doors at the end of a second hall opened into a large room. There must've been fifteen pairs of desks facing each other. Each set of desks had a printer beside a computer terminal.

Several detectives were in the room. A couple sat at their desks, working while three huddled at the end of the row of desks involved in some conversation. Daniel walked to the desk a third of the way down a row. He snagged a chair from the neighboring desk, which was unoccupied, and placed it beside his desk. "Have a seat."

Her stomach jumped as she wondered what Daniel needed to talk to her about.

"I thought we might go over some of the things that I know about Joyce, because at this point, the information Raul and I collected doesn't seem to fit together."

"I'll do what I can, but Mom might be a better source of information."

"I have some things I want to run by her, too. What do you think of Cam McGinnis?"

"He's a nice man and has always been nice to me. Mom and Dad liked him. He's also helped at the store, worked with Dad when my parents' garage flooded and helped them move items to get to the water heater."

"He's never done anything suspicious?"

"Do you mean other than lose it like he did the other day at Joyce's funeral?"

Daniel nodded. "That's exactly what I mean."

"No. His hostility that day didn't make any sense. He's usually so calm and levelheaded."

"No run-ins with the law?"

The question struck Elena funny. "Yeah, he's had a run-in with the meter maids. He parked in front of his own store and didn't put money into the meter. When he saw the cop writing the ticket, he raced out of his store, yelling his head off. We all thought his reaction was funny. But other than that, nothing."

Daniel scratched down a few notes. "What about Preston? Was it a surprise when Cam said Preston and Joyce were boyfriend-girlfriend?"

Leaning forward, she said, "It shocked me. Preston is a ladies' man, flirting with any woman within a hundred yards of him, no matter their age. Joyce didn't go for that sort of slick behavior." She thought for a moment. "In a way, Frank Gleason is like that. Maybe that's why she ignored Preston."

"Had she mentioned Preston at all?" he pressed.

"No. But you must remember that I only worked closely with her the last few months. And during that time, we were trying to get all the things from my father's estate straightened out."

"And she never said anything about her ex?"

"Not to me, but Mom would be able to answer that better."

He set his pen down, and his gaze met hers. "Could any of these break-ins at your store be connected to your birth family?"

She jerked back as if slapped. "What?"

He lifted a shoulder. "I need to consider all the possibilities."

"I don't think so. My birth mother is dead, and my father's still in prison for killing her."

"Is there anything about your brother that someone would object to?" he pressed.

"No. In high school, Adrian and another guy competed for the same girl, but I doubt the other boy carried that intense a grudge."

"I meant your birth brother?"

His question startled her. "Rafe? I haven't seen him since the trial. And I seriously doubt that he would break into the antique store if he wanted to contact me. Why not just come by the store and say hello?"

"Agreed. Are there any other family members, birth or adoptive, that you have? Aunts, uncles, cousins?"

"My birth father's brother lives in Albuquerque. He wasn't willing to step up to the plate and take my brother and me years ago. Why would he want to rob my adoptive parents' store now?"

"That's what I want to know," he calmly answered.

She shook her head. "I don't think Uncle Caesar would want anything to do with me since he feels like Rafe and I sent his brother to prison."

She paused and her mind wandered back to Rafe. He'd always been her protector. When her birth father started to rage after a few beers, Rafe would always tell her to go next door to her friend's house. Or leave. Or go into her room and stay in her closet until their pop would pass out drunk. Rafe had taken more than one beating to spare her from harm.

"Is that true?"

"Yes. I testified, too, but Rafe, since he was older, was more believable."

"He was a good guy," Daniel commented.

"The best. More than once, he diverted my dad from smacking me to pummeling him."

"What happened?" Daniel's eyes and voice drew her, wanting her to confide in him.

"We were split in foster care. After Dad's trial, Rafe seemed to fall off the face of the earth. I haven't seen him in seventeen years. But, again, if he wanted to see me, he'd not break into the shop."

"I agree, but give me his full name. I can check it out."

"His name if Rafael Cortez Segura. He's in his early thirties now. We were both born in Las Vegas, New Mexico."

Often she'd wondered what had happened to Rafe. For months after the trial, she longed to see him. When Phillip and Diane had adopted her she had wanted Adrian to fill the hole Rafe left. But he wasn't Rafe. Adrian was laughter and teasing. His mischief was legendary. And part of his sunny personality came from living with loving parents.

Eventually, she learned it was better to close off her longing for Rafe and live in the here and now.

"I think that's all I needed to ask." Daniel put down his pen. "April's been asking about you."

Thinking of April, full of questions and thirst for knowledge, brought a smile. "What's she asking about?"

"She wanted to know more about you. Who you were, how I knew you, and if you were a suspect." He shook his head. "She was relieved that you weren't the suspect."

A chuckle bubbled up. "You tell April any time she wants to come to the shop and wander through it, I'd love to have her. As a matter of fact, my mother has this thing for spoiling girls. I know she'll spread the spoiling around to April."

"Will I be able to live with her if your mom gets hold of April?" he teased.

"Probably not. But understand that girls need some girl time to talk girl stuff."

"I believe that."

The door to the room opened and Raul walked into the room. "Sorry I'm late. I've been talking to Fred Gleason, aka Bryce Green's parole officer." He nodded to Elena.

"And…" Motioning with his hand, Daniel encouraged Raul to tell them what'd he learned.

"Since Bryce has never shown his face to his parole officer, he put out an APB. When he learned that Bryce was here, he said for us to put his b—"

Daniel glared at his partner.

"—uh, to arrest him and put him in jail immediately." He glanced at Elena. "I guess I'll talk to the watch officer and alert him to what we want. The next shift needs to know about him." Raul nodded to Elena and raced outside.

"I'm sorry about that," Daniel told Elena.

"I hope you find him." She stood and walked to the door. Daniel followed. With her hand around the doorknob, she paused. "Please consider bringing April by the shop. Her dad could even stay, and we could show him around, too. Who knows, you might like some of that old stuff."

He gave her a self-effacing grin. "You've got a date."

Oddly enough, it would be the first date she'd been looking forward to for a long time.

Daniel watched Elena walk out of the room. One of the other detectives walked by him.

"Close your mouth, Stillwater," he teased.

Daniel woke from his daze.

"I hope she's not a suspect," the detective said.

"Naw, she's the witness," Raul supplied walking back to his desk.

Daniel returned to his desk. "You warned the shift commander about Bryce?"

"Yup."

Daniel tried to lose himself in his work, but his mind kept coming back to Elena. With those few words, "bring April by the shop," she'd endeared herself to him. He knew his daughter needed a woman's touch. No matter how hard he tried, there were some things that his daughter needed a female to talk to about.

April had made a connection with Elena. That was obvious. It was as if a switch had been turned on in his daughter mentioning Elena constantly. Apparently, Elena felt a connection, too, and was willing to help with his daughter.

"Daniel," Raul called. "Earth to Daniel."

"What?" He sounded grouchy to his own ears.

Raul threw up his hand in surrender and backed away.

Daniel rubbed his hand over his face. "Sorry."

"Patrol found out where Bryce was staying. He saw them and escaped out the back door of the apartment. We need to go."

Daniel closed his program and grabbed his jacket. When he met Raul at the door to the detective's room, Raul grinned at him.

"What are you smiling at?" Daniel demanded.

"You."

"What about me?"

"My Lisa's going to love the fact that 'I-don't-want-anyone-fixin'-me-up' Stillwater has a bad case of love."

"Quit blowing smoke, Rodriguez, and let's go." Daniel marched out to their car, knowing in his heart that his partner had nailed it. His heart was involved. What was he going to do?

He slipped into the back window of Joyce's house. It wasn't hard. He landed inside the washroom, just off the kitchen. He wanted to check again the contents of the house. He hadn't finished his search when that woman showed up. Besides he could've missed something in the darkness. He walked into the kitchen and opened all the cabinets, searching. He found nothing unusual. Pulling the drawers out, he looked inside them, running his hands under the drawer to make sure nothing was taped to the bottom side.

Zilch.

He moved to the next room.

It took him twenty minutes to work his way through the house. He found nothing. Nothing.

That didn't make sense. Joyce had it. But where had she hidden it?

The front door opened.

"I hope we brought enough cleaning supplies."

"If not, I can run to the store," another female voice answered.

He needed to get out of here. He looked out the bedroom window. The drop from the second floor could be made, but the large tree inches from the window offered a better way of escape. He could slip out, and no one would be wiser. He opened the window. He yanked the screen and pulled it into the room. He launched himself and caught a tree branch. Kicking his feet, he wrapped them around the branch. He slowly worked his way toward the trunk. When he reached it, he released the limb and dropped to his feet.

"Did you hear something?" Diane asked Elena.

"No."

Diane walked to the window and looked out.

"See anything?"

"Someone ran out of the backyard," Diane answered.

Elena surveyed the mess. "You think he broke in?"

"How are we going to tell?" Diane surveyed the destruction. "Was this how it was last week?"

"Yes." Elena wandered around the first floor. Since no one had come to clean up the first mess, it was impossible to know if anything had been taken. She walked up the steps, looking into each room. In Joyce's bedroom, she found the open window and screen inside.

"Find anything?" her mom yelled up.

Elena walked into the hall. "Someone escaped out of the bedroom window."

Diane walked out of the kitchen into the living room. "Before we clean, you need to talk to the police."

Shaking her head, Elena said, "I was afraid you were going to say that."

* * *

Daniel and Raul arrived at Joyce's house within minutes of the call. They'd heard the call on the police radio.

Raul scanned the room. "Did this mess happen today?"

"No. This mess is from a few days ago," Elena answered.

His brow arched, he asked, "Then how do you know anyone was in here?"

"We heard them," Diane answered. "And there's a missing screen and open window in the upstairs bedroom."

They all walked up to the room.

"You heard the burglar jump from the tree into the backyard?" Daniel asked.

"Yes." Diane nodded her head.

They walked down the stairs. When they reached the bottom step, someone pounded on the front door. Daniel glanced out and saw the patrolmen. Icenhour and his partner stood there. When Daniel opened the door, the patrolmen stared. Quickly, Daniel explained what happened. The patrolmen took down the report and left. Crime scene unit was called.

Daniel and Raul interviewed the ladies as they waited for crime scene. The unit made it within an hour and dusted the screen. There were no usable prints on either the downstairs window or the bedroom window.

"If you discover anything else, call," Daniel told the women.

And although he included everyone, his eyes met Elena's and held for a moment. She felt the connection.

"I will."

They walked out of the house. Elena thought she heard Raul say, "You've got it bad."

Elena and Diane worked at packing up the kitchen.

A knock at the back door stopped the women. Diane answered it. Carolyn Ellis stood there.

"I'm here to help. I brought boxes and muscle." There were several of the men from the homeless shelter standing behind her.

"Okay. We've finished the kitchen and it's ready to be loaded."

Carolyn nodded and had the men start putting the boxes into the van.

"Has Frank Gleason shown up at the shelter again?" Elena asked.

"No. He's done a disappearing act." Carolyn shook her head. "He was just too good to be true."

Moving to the living room, Diane asked, "Can

you use any of this furniture?" A new sofa, a recliner, and coffee table sat across from a new twenty-seven-inch TV.

"I can."

"Good. Once the guys take all the kitchen things, they can come back for these."

Carolyn went back into the kitchen to talk to the men loading the kitchen. A short time later, Carolyn rejoined them and started packing up the room.

"When did Frank appear?" Elena asked.

Frowning, Carolyn said, "It was just before Joyce's death. She worked one evening and ran into Frank. She didn't indicate she knew him, but she left early that night."

"He was her ex-husband."

Both Carolyn and Diane stared. Carolyn opened her mouth and closed it. Diane shook her head as if she didn't hear correctly.

"How do you know?" Carolyn asked.

Elena explained what Daniel had told her.

Carolyn collapsed onto the sofa. "That makes sense."

"What do you mean, Carolyn?" Diane asked.

"Joyce acted like she didn't know the man, but later in the evening, I saw them arguing. That's when Joyce left early."

"Did you tell the cops?" Elena asked.

"No. I just now thought of it."

"That's important, Carolyn. I'd call the detective and tell them."

"This is all so unbelievable," she muttered.

"I agree. But we can't ignore the truth."

But we can't ignore the truth.

The words hit Elena like a blow to her middle. For an instant she couldn't breathe. "If you'll excuse me, I'll pack up Joyce's things."

Elena made it to Joyce's room before her legs gave way. She felt her world collapsing around her. Daniel's suggestion that Joyce's death might somehow be connected with her past made Elena reexamine her own life. Her mother's death. The trial. The loss of Rafe.

Why, Lord, is this happening?

Her mother appeared in the doorway. She walked to the bed and put her arm around her daughter. "Old nightmares are coming back, aren't they?"

"Yes. And I don't understand why the Lord is letting this happen again."

"Is this about you, Elena?"

The question jerked her out of her self-pity. She opened her mouth, but closed it again when she couldn't deny the truth.

"You've been able to walk away from the pain

and torment of your mother's death. Don't go back there, child. Rest in the Lord."

"How?"

"You trust that He will keep His Word. You've walked out of that nightmare. Don't let it overtake you again. Remember Daniel in the Old Testament. He found himself in a foreign land, with countless bad things happening to him. But he trusted God in each trial and God never left Daniel. Each time, food from the king's table, bowing down to worship the idol, being thrown into the fiery furnace, Daniel trusted. He didn't ask God why he was being tested again. He trusted.

"God's brought you through one horror. He'll bring you though this. And who knows what lives you will touch. What of April Stillwater? You can minister to that child in a way none of us can. I grieve for Joyce. I don't know why she was murdered, or why she had to die. But we know Who has control over this situation and our lives."

Elena rested her head on her mother's shoulder. Diane and Phillip Jackson were rocks of stability that she would always be thankful for. They were a refuge of peace. But more than that, they taught her how to rest in the Lord in the midst of the storm.

"Diane," Carolyn called out. "We've got a problem."

"What?" Diane answered as they hurried into the hall. When they looked down into the living room, they saw Frank Gleason.

He was holding a gun on Carolyn.

EIGHT

"Why don't you ladies join us down here?" Frank commanded, motioning them down the stairs.

Elena's mind raced. "Why?"

"This is not question and answer time. Move it." He motioned with the gun.

They hurried down the stairs.

"Sit." He jabbed the gun toward the sofa.

As she sat, Elena thought about the cell phone in her pocket. Maybe she could press the button for the operator. It was worth a try.

"Now, I want to ask you ladies if you've found my money."

"What money?" Elena demanded.

"The money that my ex-wife hid after I was arrested."

Elena glanced at her mother. Elena knew nothing of this so-called money, but then again, there were lots of things she didn't know about Joyce.

"Well," he demanded again, stepping toward Carolyn.

Elena slipped her hand into her pocket of her sweater. Running her forefinger over the buttons, she punched 911.

"Why would I know?"

The connection opened up, and Elena held the speaker to her body to muffle the operator's voice.

He turned to them. "Since she worked for you—" he nodded to Diane "—she probably told you where she kept my money."

"There was never any mention of money," Diane calmly answered.

Elena turned over the phone, praying the operator would hear.

"Joyce worked for you since she got out of prison. She probably made up some story about her worthless husband who got her sent to prison."

"No. She didn't mention anything about you."

He stepped back and looked around the room.

Elena slipped the phone out of her pocket and put it behind her back.

He looked around the room for something. Suddenly, they heard an engine—probably the truck, pulling into the driveway.

Motioning toward Carolyn, he said, "You go outside and tell whoever is out there to leave."

Carolyn disappeared into the kitchen. From her vantage point on the sofa, Elena could see the table and chairs through the archway, but Carolyn had walked to the back door where she couldn't see her. Frank leaned against the wall and tried to catch a glimpse of the man Carolyn was talking with.

"Hey, guys. We're still not finished here."

Elena looked around the living room for a route of escape. She saw, much to her surprise, her mother pick up a small vase. Elena wanted to shout for her to be careful.

"We can help you pack, Carolyn."

Her mother stepped closer. When Frank caught a glimpse of movement out of his eye, he turned, but Diane was quicker and broke the vase over his head. He staggered back against the wall. The gun discharged, grazing Diane's forehead.

Elena raced at him and grabbed his arm, trying to slam it into the wall. He punched her in the jaw and the world went black for her.

When she opened her eyes, an EMS worker stood over her. Daniel stood behind him.

"How's Mom?" The words popped out of her mouth.

The EMS worker nodded. He held a capsule in his hands. "She's fine."

She looked at Daniel. "Tell me."

"Her wound was minor, but she's been taken to the hospital."

Elena tried to get up, but the world tilted. The EMS worker caught her.

"Try to get up slowly."

Daniel knelt beside her. "Give yourself a moment to get your bearings."

She didn't want to be babied but realized that landing in the emergency room, too, wouldn't help her mother. Sitting, she allowed the world to settle into its correct place.

"Did he get away?" Elena asked.

"Yes," Daniel answered. "By the time the cops got here, he'd escaped out the front. Carolyn's guys raced after him, but he disappeared."

The paramedic closed his EMT kit and stood. "If you have any headaches in the next few days, go to the emergency room and have yourself checked out."

He left.

Daniel helped her to her feet. "Let me take you home."

"No. I'm going to the hospital." She walked to the back door. He caught up with her and grasped her elbow. She looked down at his hand. "What are you doing?"

"You shouldn't be driving yourself. I'll take you."

Elena admitted to herself that she was in no condition to drive. "All right. Take me to the hospital."

Once in the car, the fear in her stomach turned into a rock. She felt so cold.

Daniel covered her hand with his. The warmth of his touch penetrated through her fear and cold. Her gaze met his.

"That was smart of you to dial 911. The operator knew immediately you were in trouble. It took a couple of minutes to figure out where the cell signal was coming from."

"It wasn't enough. Mom shouldn't have been the one to take him out. I should've protected her."

"Elena, don't second-guess yourself."

She grasped on to his words like a life preserver. The past horror of watching her birth mother die was mirrored in today's events.

"What did he say?"

"He said that Joyce had his money. And he wanted it. He acted as if we should've known what he was talking about."

"But he didn't give you any kind of idea about

this money. Where it was or if it was cash or maybe jewelry?"

"He only said money. Now from what I've seen of Joyce's house, she didn't have a lot of extra cash. I haven't searched every inch of her house, but there's nothing that I've seen of great value."

He turned into the hospital parking lot. "Did she have a safety deposit box?"

"I don't know. You'll have to ask Mom."

He parked and walked into the E.R. with her. Elena raced to the admitting desk and was led back to a curtained section of the E.R. Diane Jackson sat in a chair by the bed. Elena ran to her mother and knelt by her side. "Are you okay?"

"I am."

The doctor stepped in and explained that Diane was fine. There would be no follow-up, except with her own doctor. Elena helped her mother stand and they walked slowly to Daniel's car.

It was only an eleven-minute trip from the hospital to the Jackson home. Daniel helped Diane into the house.

"I'd like to take some of that pain medicine the doctor gave me and lie down," Diane informed them. She walked into her room. Elena followed. The fear she'd lose another mother to violence ate at her soul.

She helped her mother change into her night-gown and brought her the pain medicine and water to take it.

"I'm okay, sweetheart," Diane reassured her. "Why don't you talk to the detective?"

Elena reluctantly left the room.

By the time she got to the living room, her hands shook.

"Is everything okay?" Daniel asked.

A tear ran down her cheek.

He stepped close and wrapped his arms around her. The fear and emotional roller coaster of the afternoon hit her.

"It's okay to cry, Elena."

"When that man turned the gun on Mom…it was the awful nightmare of my past being relived. Only this time I would not stand by and watch my mother be k-killed." She gave in to the terror racing through her veins.

Daniel felt his heart jerk in sympathy. Her reaction back at Joyce's house wasn't that out-landish, but considering her past, he realized what a traumatic episode it had been. As far as he was concerned, she'd done a good job of handling herself. She shouldn't be so hard on herself. "You didn't stand back and do nothing."

"I shou-should've done something more."

"Elena, you stopped him."

"Mom did that."

His hands slipped to her shoulders, and he put his finger under her chin. "I think you're trying to assume a power you don't have."

Through puzzled, watery eyes she looked at him. "What?"

"You are not God. Why are you trying to assume His power?"

"No. That's not what I'm doing."

"But it is. You couldn't read your mother's mind, and you did act when you saw her."

She shook her head.

"It's a hard lesson, Elena, and I learned it through experience. When I was with my army unit, some of my men were wounded and killed. I blamed myself for every death, every mishap. I should've protected them. Seen the bomb in the car. Seen the sniper. I was trying to assume the all-knowing, all-seeing power. But God doesn't require that of me. He asks me to be faithful. Prepare my men the best I can. Lead them, but it's not my responsibility to see the future."

He thought of the young private under his command who had walked by the car parked on the street in Kandahar when it had blown up. The young man lost both legs. When he went to the hospital to visit him, the young man placed no blame on him. He'd simply asked Daniel to write his mother and tell her that he'd be fine. He'd nearly lost it there. Later, when he asked God why it had happened, Daniel realized that it wasn't his job to mold the future, but to prepare his men for the fight.

"It's a hard lesson to learn."

She dried her eyes. "Do you still blame yourself?"

"No. But I will tell you that I grieve for those young men who didn't come home. Or came home wounded."

She stepped back and grabbed a tissue from the box on the end table and blew her nose. The sound made him smile. Her eyes met his.

"As Oprah says, I was into the ugly cry."

"Is that what she says?"

She nodded.

"Don't blame yourself. It will cripple you."

A shy smile curved her lips. "Thank you."

He cupped her cheek. His thumb glided over her smooth skin. "I'm thankful that both you and your mother are okay."

He stopped himself from brushing his lips over hers, but it took all the willpower he could muster.

He didn't remember the drive home. He stopped at Rosalyn's house to pick up his daughter. She chatted about her day, about the stupid boy at school who threw lunch meat at her. Every word she uttered brought joy to his soul.

April didn't stop talking as they made dinner and did homework. When he kissed her good-night, she smiled a little-girl smile that melted his core.

He should've been here for Nita. It had taken her getting breast cancer to bring him home. Although, he knew her illness hadn't been his fault, his heart didn't accept the logic.

Nita hadn't blamed him for her illness. Those last days, they reestablished the relationship that they enjoyed when they first wed. She'd forgiven him his desertion of her and that had driven an arrow into his chest. He'd lived with that guilt since he buried her. But the words he'd just said to Elena hit him hard. *Don't blame yourself. It will cripple you.*

Those words reverberated in his soul.

He walked to April's room and looked at his sleeping daughter. He felt a peace. And a freedom. He'd been forgiven for his mistakes. He let go of the guilt.

"Thank you, Lord, for my April. I'll do my best not to fail her."

NINE

Daniel pulled up to Past Treasures and killed the engine. When the report came in this morning that Past Treasures had been broken into again, he'd been in court testifying about another murder case. Raul had been in Roswell attending the parole hearing of his brother's murderer.

The report had been taken at eight-thirty this morning. It was now six-fifteen. The day had been wasted in court. The prosecutor hadn't called him today. Daniel had simply sat in court while the defense tap-danced around with the D.A. over plea negotiations. It had gone in fits and starts, with the defense finally throwing in the towel about four this afternoon. They pled down to second-degree murder. When Daniel had gone into the office, the watch commander had put on his desk the incident report for the break-in this morning.

He walked in the door and tried the handle. It opened. The sign on the door said the shop closed at five.

That unnerved him, and he planned to deliver a lecture to Ms. Jackson. Safety first, last, and everything in between.

Once inside, his gaze immediately went to Elena, who was carting a large unwieldy box up the stairs.

"What are you doing?" he barked.

She swung around and the box slipped out of her hands and tumbled down the stairs. She followed, careening down a couple of steps.

Daniel raced across the room and took the steps two at a time. They crashed into each other midway down. Her momentum staggered him, but he was able to catch himself on the railing, pulling her close to his body.

The box crashed into an old metal pot. It rolled and smashed into a seventeenth-century Spanish spice chest, knocking it off the display table. Papers and small items went flying everywhere.

When the noise stopped and the papers settled on the floor, he looked into her eyes. "Are you all right?"

He could see the fear receding in her eyes. "What are you doing scaring me like that?"

"Me? What are you doing with the front door open? Anyone could've walked in and with the problems you've been having, you need to be more cautious."

Her gaze slid from his and he knew he made his point. "I just bought some items from a young woman who wanted to sell her grandfather's things. He'd just passed away, and she wanted to clear out his things. I picked up the box and was carrying it upstairs."

"And you left the front door open?"

Her gaze slid from his. "I was trying to hurry home."

He still held her, felt the warmth of her body seep through the chilling fear surrounding his heart. He cupped her face between his hands. "You need to be more careful." He ran his thumbs over her cheeks. His actions were completely out of character, but the need to protect her overrode all other instincts.

Her eyes widened, then drifted to his lips. He closed the distance and softly brushed his lips over hers. It wasn't enough. He settled his mouth over hers and tasted the sweetness of this special woman.

When he broke away, he rested his forehead on hers. "I shouldn't have done that."

"Why?"

"Because you're a witness in a criminal investigation."

"Oh."

He gave her one last quick kiss, dropped his hand and stepped away. He shouldn't have kissed her, though oddly enough, he didn't regret it. But it couldn't happen again.

Running his fingers through his hair, he tried to refocus on why he was here. "I've been in court all day. When I got to my desk and read that your store had been broken into, I came immediately. Tell me what happened."

"When we came into the shop this morning, the alarm system had been disabled and the back door unlocked." She shrugged.

"Elena, whoever is breaking in is looking for something. Probably something Joyce had. They are not going to let you stop them."

She didn't meet his eyes. Instead, she stared at his shirt buttons. "I was simply bringing things into the store."

"What's going on here?"

They broke apart and looked down into Cam's frowning face. "Are you all right, Elena?"

Her cheeks turned bright red. "I am."

He looked around at the mess on the floor. The spice chest with its drawers scattered over the floor and the papers in the box looked like a dusting of snow inside the shop. He rested his fists on his hips. "What happened?"

Shrugging, she said, "The detective surprised me."

Cam glared at him. The more Daniel was around Cam McGinnis, the less he liked him.

"What are you doing scaring her like that?" Cam demanded.

The ex-hippie had used up all his free punches. "What exactly are you doing here?" Daniel shot back.

"I was working on a piece of jewelry a woman ordered yesterday. I need it finished by tomorrow."

Elena moved down the stairs. "Daniel wanted to check on me after the break-in this morning."

"Again?" Cam frowned.

"You didn't know about that?" Daniel asked.

A muscle in his jaw flexed. "I'd driven to Taos to pick up several stones for this necklace. I didn't arrive at the shop until the afternoon."

They were at a standoff. Cam wasn't going to back down. Daniel didn't feel as though he wanted to soothe Mr. Prickly.

Elena solved the problem. She took Cam's arm and stared walking him to the door. "Thank you for checking on me. You're a good neighbor."

He glanced at Daniel. "You sure you're okay? You don't need me to stay and help with this mess?" He nodded toward the scattered papers and items from the box.

"You need to finish your project. I'll only be a few minutes before I lock up. I think the detective will watch over me until I leave."

McGinnis gave him a look that said he doubted the cops could do anything right.

Elena leaned close and brushed his cheek with a kiss. "Thank you."

Cam looked at Elena. "If you're sure."

"I am."

He glared at Daniel, then walked out of the shop.

Daniel joined her on the ground floor.

"He's been very protective of Mom and me." She turned and started toward the spice chest. "I appreciate his concern and help."

Daniel picked up one of the small drawers from the spice chest. She snagged several of the other drawers. As she reached for the body of the spice chest, Daniel noticed that the last drawer, which was twice as long as the others, hadn't spilled out. She put in the drawer she held and the one Daniel offered her.

She tried to push the long drawer back in, but it wouldn't close. "What—"

She struggled to pull out the drawer. With a yank, it came lose, and she stumbled back. He caught her and took the chest from her hand. They looked at the drawer, discovering several papers stuffed into it.

"What's that?" Daniel asked.

"I don't know." She pulled out the papers and looked over them. "It's a verification document."

"Did you have it done?"

"It's not for this chest." She handed him the drawer. "These are papers from Real Deal Art Experts. They were asked to evaluate a painting, *Toreador at the Kill*." She turned it over, but the report was not attached.

"And you never handled this painting?"

"No. I've never seen that painting, but—I think Preston had such a painting in his gallery."

He took the paper from her and read it. "Then why is it here, stuffed in this spice chest?"

"Good question," Elena replied.

"Do you think that the other sheet might have fallen out?"

Scanning the mess on the floor, she shrugged. "There's no way to tell unless we search the other sheets."

He began to pick up the papers.

"That's not necessary."

"It is, Elena, for two reasons. First, it might be a clue to why Joyce was murdered. And second, if you think I'll walk out that door and leave you to clear this up by yourself, then you're sadly mistaken."

Reading the intent in his eyes, she nodded. "Thank you."

There was so much more he wanted to say to her, but now wasn't the time.

Together, they picked up all the loose paper covering the floor. It took close to an hour to gather all the papers and review each sheet.

Shaking her head, she said, "It's not here."

He thought about the report. "Why would Preston have this done?" he asked. "Is that unusual?"

"No. It's not uncommon to have a documented painting re-certified to make sure it hasn't been stolen or hasn't been forged. It's not uncommon to have a copy of the real thing and to keep the original under lock and key. Several years ago there was a big scandal where several famous museums in Europe were displaying forgeries without knowing it."

"So Preston could've had this painting evaluated as a matter of practice?"

"Yes. Some of the pieces we handle have to have an art expert's stamp of approval. It's part of doing business. It's the same with paintings. And famous pieces of jewelry have to have a paper history. Even show dogs have their documentation. If you have any questions, you can ask Preston."

"Did I hear my name mentioned?" Preston stood inside the doorway of the shop.

"What are you doing here?" Elena asked.

His brow arched. "I'd locked up and was driving by the front of your shop and saw the cars. I was worried with all that has gone on." From his tone and raised chin, the man was offended. "I was watching out for my neighbor."

Daniel didn't like the man just barging into the shop. But Cam had also made an unexpected visit. Elena either had concerned neighbors or possible suspects.

Elena set the papers on the table and stood. She and Daniel had sat on an old Spanish settee and looked at all the papers. She hurried to Preston's side. "And I appreciate your concern. It's our good neighbors who make me feel safe."

"But you told him to ask me. What did you want to know?"

Elena opened her mouth, but Daniel caught her eye and shook his head. Her eyes widened, but she closed her mouth.

"You remember my partner's comment about that painting the other day?" Daniel said, filling the void.

"Yes."

"Well, the guys downtown wanted to get him a gag gift. I was wondering if I could take a picture of that painting and blow it up to give him as a gag birthday present?"

Preston's eyes widened. "You want to use my Jaunes as a gag gift? My priceless painting?" He stiffened his spine and looked down his nose at Daniel. An outraged rooster had nothing on Preston Jones.

Elena stared at Preston with her mouth wide-open.

"No. You'll have to think of some other way to needle your partner." He turned to Elena. "Would you like for me to stay until you leave?" He glanced at Daniel. "We wouldn't want anything to happen to you."

She blinked and shook her head. "Thank you, Preston, for your concern. I will be all right with the detective."

"I don't know. Up to this point, all that has happened is they've chased their tails. They've not stopped the break-ins or caught the murderer."

Daniel knew exactly what Jones was doing, goading him. The man in him wanted to go a few rounds with the self-important Jones, but the detective in him knew better.

"Preston, I am surprised at you," Elena chastened him.

He looked down at her. "I'm sorry. The detective has no appreciation of art."

She swallowed her smile. "Sometimes people don't. You and I know that. You ignore it."

"You're right." He started for the door, then stopped. "I thought you should know. Earlier today there was a man taking pictures of your shop. When I went to talk to him, he disappeared."

"What did he look like?" Elena asked.

"In his early thirties, five-eleven, slim. He was shooting the store from across the street between the buildings. When I went outside to confront him, he disappeared."

A chill ran up her back. "Thank you."

He nodded and left.

Elena turned back to Daniel. "What's going on?" Her voice quavered.

Crossing the room, he took her hands. They were cold. "I don't know, Elena. There are too many things going on that seem random. But that very randomness makes me uneasy."

"Why didn't you want me to tell Preston about the papers?"

"Because, I don't want Preston to know anything about this."

"Do you suspect him of doing something?"

"At this point, Elena, I'm considering all the possibilities. I think I want to talk to this art expert before I talk to Jones."

She frowned. "Are you sure?"

"I am. I'll get in contact with Real Deal Experts and see who did this estimation."

"I could call for you. I deal with them all the time."

"You know them?"

"I know several of the people there since we use them for verification all the time."

"Okay, why don't I drop by here tomorrow right after you open. Then you can call."

She nodded.

He watched as the detective and Elena left the shop. They were getting too close. He didn't like it. Everything had gone south and no matter what he did, things continued to get worse. What he wanted to know was why Joyce decided to be the morality police. If she'd just kept her nose out of this business, none of this would be happening now.

And he wouldn't let it happen again. Maybe he should leave Elena a little message. That might stop her.

TEN

"**I**'d like to speak to Felix Glaser," Elena told the receptionist as she clutched the phone. Elena looked up at Daniel, who stood behind her chair. He'd shown up at the shop exactly at nine this morning for her to call Real Deal Art Experts.

"He's not answering his phone. Would you like his voice mail?"

"Yes." She left the message. When she hung up, she turned to Daniel, who leaned against the desk. "Felix's not there. Would you like for me to talk to the other appraiser I use?"

Rubbing his neck, he thought about her question. "Yeah, let's see if we can determine why Preston wanted the appraisal on the painting."

Elena had dealt with Carrie Nash, a young woman who'd only been with that appraisal company for a few years. She'd hit it off with the woman since they'd both worked at Christie's. She dialed the number and got Carrie on the line.

"I'm trying to contact Felix about some work he did with Preston Jones here in Santa Fe. I found some papers in my store about a painting. I want to talk to Felix about what I found."

Daniel's brow rose. She felt her face flush.

"I don't know anything about that. But it is strange. Felix hasn't shown up for work for the last few days."

Elena looked at Daniel. "He didn't call in sick or have a trip planned?"

"No. I had a question about a piece of art that a woman brought to me. A painting. She claimed it was a Gerard Dou. Since Felix is an expert in seventeenth-century Dutch masters, I wanted to ask him some questions. He's not been in."

"Thanks, Carrie." She hung up.

Rolling his shoulders, he said, "I don't like the look on your face."

"Apparently, the man who evaluated the painting is missing."

Pushing away from the desk, he paced the small space. "Remember I told you the randomness of the things happening wasn't right. This only adds to it."

"It could be he decided to—run off." She blushed. It sounded stupid.

"It's a possibility, but I doubt it."

"It's strange that he would disappear so close to Joyce's death and us finding…"

"I don't think coincidence plays a part in this."

A chill ran up her spine. "I don't get a good feeling about this."

He stopped by her chair. "I think you might have another career, Ms. Jackson."

"Why do you say that?"

"Because good detectives develop a sixth sense, so to speak. Maybe it's dealing with life-and-death issues, but they depend on that internal sense of what's happening."

"Well, you can keep your job. I prefer to deal with antiques."

He walked out of the office. She trailed him. At the store's front door, he asked, "How's your mother feeling?"

"She's fine. She plans on coming back to work today."

"But you're worried."

She wrapped her arms around her waist. "I want this to end, Daniel. Why won't this nightmare end?"

"I can't say. Whatever is going on is, I believe, connected with Joyce's death."

He'd voiced what she'd feared.

"I think everything will be okay for you and your mother. I'll make sure that the patrols around this area check on you. I'll try to be back here at closing time."

"You don't have to do that."

He stepped closer. "I want to, Elena. This case has become very personal for me. I've come to care for some of the people involved."

Her breath caught. She read from the dark intensity of his eyes, he meant every word.

She wanted to answer, but she couldn't put voice to the emotions in her heart. She touched his cheek. "Thank you," she whispered.

He brushed his mouth over hers. "I'll be back."

She smiled. "You sound like a very famous person."

"Trust me, I mean every word."

Back in his office, Daniel dialed the number of the Albuquerque PD and asked for Jonathan Littledeer. Jon and Daniel had been in the same unit in the army. They'd seen combat in Afghanistan.

"Stillwater. Good to hear from you. This a social call or business?"

"I've got a problem, Jon, that I hope you can help me with." He went on to explain about the missing man. "I think the man is legit. But something might have happened to him. It's connected with a murder here in Santa Fe. Would you check around for me?"

"Sure. I'll let you know what I find out. I was sorry to hear about your wife."

That little stab of guilt that usually accompanied thoughts of his wife didn't appear. He could think of Nita without sadness. "Thanks, Jon." He hung up the phone and sat staring at it, amazed at the change. He'd released the guilt.

What truly amazed him was that he could think of Nita, his actions, and their marriage without pain and guilt.

He'd taken his own advice and prayed, giving it to God. *The peace that passes all understanding.* Those words were a living truth he knew.

Raul walked into the detectives' room. "Any progress on the Murphy murder?"

Daniel filled his partner in on what he'd discovered at Elena's yesterday.

Leaning back in his chair, he laced his hands behind his head. "So why was this evaluation stuffed into the spice box at Past Treasures?"

"I don't know. That's why I wanted to talk to the appraiser. He has a history with Jones."

Raul unclasped his hand and ran his palm over his face. "And the appraiser is missing?"

"It doesn't sound good." That's what troubled Daniel. He didn't know if his confusion came from his feelings for Elena or that the case was still so opaque. "And Jones told us about the person taking pictures of Elena's shop. When Jones tried to question him, the man disappeared. What do you think is going on there?"

"I don't know. It sounds like we've got another player in this mess."

"And added to this chaos, there's Cam McGinnis, who hates all cops and probably wouldn't volunteer the truth if he knew it. And there's Joyce's ex-husband, who's been sneaking around the city."

"We could send Detective Martinez undercover to talk to McGinnis." Raul grinned.

Loretta Martinez could hold her own against any suspect. And nothing gets by that sharp lady.

"I like your idea. Why don't we call her and ask for a favor."

"Just be ready to be tapped when she needs help," Raul reminded.

"Anything."

"Hey, partner, you eaten?" Raul asked as he walked up to their desks.

Daniel glanced at his watch. One forty-seven.

He leaned back against his chair, stretching. "I didn't realize it was so late."

"Then c'mon, let's go get something to eat."

Daniel stood. The phone on his desk rang. He wanted to ignore it, but he jerked it off its cradle. "Stillwater."

"What, are you going for the big, bad cop imitation?" Jon Littledeer asked.

"No. I'm just a hungry man on his way to lunch."

"Then I'll make this brief, buddy. I asked patrol to send someone over to Felix Glasner's house. No one answered, so he peeked into the window. There had been some sort of struggle in the living room. When he tried the door, it opened. He called it in, then walked inside. We may have a kidnapping. When he walked through the house, everything else was in order. We put out an APB for the missing man."

Daniel rubbed the back of his neck. "Did the patrolman think there was any foul play?"

"There was no blood, if that's what you're asking."

"Thanks, Jon. Let me know if you come up with anything else."

When Daniel hung up, he looked at his partner. "Looks like our art expert might be in some trouble. Let's go and I'll explain what Jon told me."

* * *

Elena picked up the phone and called Preston's shop. "Hey, Preston, I'm going to need your help. Yesterday afternoon, I was called to an estate to remove some pieces. I have a painting I'd like for you to look at."

"Sure, I can do that. How about I come after we close? I'm expecting several clients this afternoon and you know how inconsiderate some of them are, never arriving at the proper time."

"Sounds good." She hung up the phone and called Cam. Again, she had several pieces of jewelry in the collection, but she recognized a piece out of the twenties that was very unusual. "Cam, I need your help." She explained the situation to him and he promised to come tonight, also.

The afternoon passed quickly. Preston showed up at five after six. She let him into the shop. Diane was with Elena.

"Diane, should you be here?" Preston asked.

"I'm fine."

Elena shook her head. "Mom, go home. You look exhausted. Preston's here with me. Also, Cam promised to come over and see about that jewelry. I'll be fine."

Diane hesitated, then nodded. "I am feeling a little weak." She gathered her purse and left.

"The painting's upstairs." They walked to the office. The box of papers she'd spilled sat in a corner. The painting rested up against the box. "This is it."

The canvas, eight inches by eleven inches, was done in the style of DeGrazia. The scene depicted a sunrise over the mesas around Taos. A single deer posed in the corner watching the dawn.

The signature, A. Mendoza, was scrawled across the right corner of the canvas.

Preston looked up, his eyes wide. "I've seen only one other of his paintings."

"I've never heard of him."

"He painted during the Depression. His settings were of New Mexico and Southern Colorado. Sold most of his works for a few dollars. He was noticed when a famous art collector fell in love with his work. He enjoyed a year or two of fame before he died of a heart attack. Although his body of work was limited, what does exist is worth a lot."

"What are we talking, Preston?"

"I don't know. In a good auction, a hundred thou. You have connections with Christie's. Call them." He handed her back the picture.

Her head spun. "I think the daughter didn't realize what she sold me."

He shrugged. "If that's the real thing, you're not obligated to fork over any money."

His comment grated on her nerves.

"I guess I'll have to call The Real Deal. Who do you use to authenticate your paintings? I could contact that person."

He seemed to tighten up. "I use several different people. Anyone in the art department will be able to give you the information you're after."

"Are you sure?"

"I am. Try any of them. And I'm telling you, if you want to use my gallery to sell that, I have connections to people who would love to buy that painting. I'd only want a small fee for the name."

Elena didn't know if her violent reaction was because Preston had so cavalierly offered his services or because he had refused to give her Felix's name. "I'll keep that in mind. Thank you for your help."

He jerked back, not expecting her obvious displeasure. Quickly, he covered his surprise. "If I can be of any further service, Elena, don't hesitate to call."

The front doorbell chimed. Elena stood and walked down the stairs. Cam stood just inside the door.

"I'm sorry I'm late. Had a bit of banking to finish."

Elena waved him upstairs. "I have some jewelry I want you to look at."

He limped up to the office.

"Are you okay? What happened?"

He blushed. "I just dropped my chisel on my foot. It's nothing."

She nodded and dug in the box that held the papers and pulled out two bracelets. They were both plastic. She held them out. Cam took them.

"I think these are out of the twenties."

Cam carefully looked at the two items. "You're right. In the twenties, Woolworth decided all women should have access to jewelry. This plastic bracelet—" he pointed to the orange bracelet "—is worth about three hundred dollars. The lime-green one is worth about eight hundred. It was the new color and all the rage.

"What made this more valuable was Jean Harlow wore it in one of her movies. I've got a few catalogs of early twentieth-century jewelry. If you want to borrow the book, I'd be happy to lend it to you."

"Thanks." She studied the box on the floor. The receipt they ran across last night was carefully hidden in her tax files. But who could've known her trip to Chimayo northeast of Santa Fe would've been so profitable? "I'm still stunned at the treasure I ran across yesterday."

"Meaning?" Cam prompted.

"You remember that mess on the floor. These bracelets and this picture—" she motioned to the small painting leaning against the box "—by A. Mendoza came from the estate of an elderly man. His daughter sold it to me for five thousand. I got a couple of old pieces of furniture from the house. I also took away this box."

"That's amazing, Elena." He gave her a thumbs-up. "If you need any other help, ask."

Preston glared at Cam.

"I need to go, too," Preston added. "My offer is still open, Elena, if you choose to use it."

"Thank you." She locked the front door after Cam and Preston left. She checked the back door to make sure that everything was locked. She walked up to her office, ready to finish the day's receipts, when the phone rang. She picked it up. "Hello."

"Elena, this is April Stillwater."

Hearing the little girl's voice shocked Elena. "How are you doing, April?"

"I was wondering if you'd like to come and have dinner tomorrow night with Dad, Grandma and me. It's my birthday, and Grandma's going to make her special enchiladas for me. And a birthday cake."

"April, your birthday's tomorrow?"

"It is. I'll be nine."

The invitation touched Elena. She had been a week shy of her ninth birthday when her father killed her mother. For the first time, her mother had convinced her father to allow her to have a party. A party that never happened. "Thank you for the lovely invitation, but I don't want to barge in on your party. I'm sure you want your school buddies there."

"Dad's going to have a party for me on Saturday with all my friends from school and church, but this dinner is for special people. Would you come, please?"

Elena was sure that Daniel didn't know that his daughter had invited her to dinner. "Have you discussed this with your father?"

"He said I could invite anyone I wanted tomorrow."

"Surely he meant for you to have one of your friends."

"He said whoever I wanted," she informed her. "I'd like you to come."

She couldn't say no and deny that beautiful little girl her wish. "I'd be delighted to come."

A little girl's shriek of delight filled Elena's ear. "I'm so glad. And you'll love coming and tasting Grandma's cooking. She's teaching me."

"I will look forward to it."

"Come at seven tomorrow night." April gave her the address.

"I'll be there," Elena promised.

Bryce Green waited in the alley, watching for the man to come out of his shop. They had some things to discuss. The door to Past Treasure's opened, and Elena walked out. After locking her store, she got into her car. His mark came out of his shop.

"Good night," he yelled at Elena.

She pulled out of her parking spot and left the alley. His quarry got in his black Caddy, pulled out of his parking space and started for the alley entrance. Bryce stepped in his way. The car stopped.

"What's the matter with you? Have a death wish? Move," the man yelled.

Bryce shrugged his shoulders. "Sure. I'll jog down to the police station and let them know that I saw a black car with the license plate CDR-457 roaring out of the alley behind Past Treasures the night Joyce Murphy was murdered. I'm sure they'd love to talk to me."

The man's eyes narrowed and his jaw muscles flexed.

"You're bluffing."

"You hope, but it's too bad for you that I was coming to see Joyce that night. She had something of mine that I wanted back."

The man in the car studied him. "What do you want?"

"I need some help. I figured we could help each other. You're in a pinch and so am I."

The man continued to glare at him. Bryce shrugged and started to turn away.

"Get in."

Bryce hid his smile of triumph. He'd hooked him. Turning, he walked around the vehicle and got into the passenger seat. The car roared off.

ELEVEN

Elena looked down at Daniel's business card. She needed to warn him about his daughter's invitation. Showing up at his house without warning him was totally out of the question.

"Why do you have the detective's card?" Diane asked her. "Did something happen after I left the shop?" The clock on the stove read seven-thirty.

A delighted smile spread across Elena's mouth. "Yeah, but it's not what you think. I got a call from April Stillwater."

"Oh?" Diane sat down at the kitchen table next to Elena.

"It seems I've been invited to a birthday party."

Diane cocked her head. "Whose?"

"April's. She called and asked if I would come to her birthday dinner that her grandmother is cooking for her." She fell silent. "She's going to be nine."

Elena didn't need to say anything more. Diane knew the meaning of that birthday for Elena. Her mother's death.

"What did you say?"

"I tried to reason my way out, but April Stillwater is a force to be reckoned with. You would appreciate it." Elena fingered the business card. "I believe I should warn Daniel before I show up."

Diane's hand covered hers. "I know you don't want to hurt April, but are you sure you want to do this?"

Tenderness, gratitude and love welled in Elena's heart. Diane still fought to protect her child. "I am, Mom, but—some way, somehow, April's heart calls to me. I know her mother's death was totally different from my mother's, but sorrow doesn't have a label. It hurts. You and Dad comforted me with such tenderness that I might be able to say something for April.

"I don't mean that Daniel isn't doing a good job, but—" she shrugged her shoulders "—sometimes a girl needs to talk to another girl."

Squeezing her hand, Diane leaned over and brushed a kiss across Elena's check. "Call him. He needs to be warned." Diane stood and left the kitchen.

Elena flipped open her cell phone and dialed the number on the card.

"Stillwater."

The man certainly didn't have the kind of voice she'd call welcoming. "Am I calling at a bad time?" she asked.

"Elena? Is everything all right?"

"Yes. Fine. I'm at home."

"Okay. Did you remember something important about Joyce?"

Things were going from bad to worse. "Uh, no. It's got nothing to do with the case."

"So why did you call?"

Her brain seemed to go blank. "I...I'm coming to your daughter's birthday dinner tomorrow. She called me at work and invited me." There, she'd said it.

Silence.

"I thought I should warn you before I showed up."

"I appreciate it." His tone remained neutral.

"I'd feel funny just showing up. Now, I assure you that this was your daughter's idea completely. I tried to talk her out of it, but she's a very determined young lady."

He laughed and the sound eased her soul.

"I have discovered that fact. And I don't blame you. I'm glad you're coming."

That was hard to believe. "Then I'll see you tomorrow night at seven."

"Until then."

She hung up the phone. He hadn't known what April had done, but recovered quickly. She turned off her cell and put it back in her purse.

Now the question was, what did you get a precocious nine-year-old for her birthday?

Daniel walked into his daughter's room. He sat on the bed and pulled out the drawer on the nightstand. Her children's Bible rested there. "Where did we stop yesterday?"

"Jesus was calming the storm. That's in Mark."

This child of his still amazed him. Daily, she revealed new things about herself. "You are right. That was Mark 4:39."

"You know, if I'd been in that boat with Jesus, I wouldn't have been worried. I know He can do all things."

Cupping her cheek, he said, "I don't doubt it."

"Jesus was with his disciplines. It didn't matter that it was raining. Jesus was there."

Truth from the mouth of babes. "You're right."

She smiled and snuggled down under her covers. He read Mark 5 to her, they prayed and when they finished, he brushed a hand over her hair.

"I got an interesting call from Elena. It seems she's coming to your birthday party."

He could feel her tensing up. "I asked her to come." She stared at their clasped hands. "She seems to understand me." She glanced up through her lashes.

The cry of April's soul touched him. She'd lost her mother but had done an amazing job of dealing with the loss. He wasn't so selfish to deny his daughter the comfort she took from Elena. "I'm glad for that, but she surprised me when she called and told me she was coming to your party at Grandma Rosalyn's."

"Well, I thought you might tell me she was too old."

He grinned.

"I don't object to your inviting her, just next time, please tell your papa."

She shot up and wrapped her arms around his waist. "Thanks, Dad."

His hand covered her head and stroked it. When she pulled back, he kissed her forehead.

"You need to warn your grandmother that you've invited someone."

"I will."

He stood and walked to the door of her room. April happily snuggled back down into her bed.

He turned off the light and started down the hall. He knew he'd lost that round with April.

He smiled. The child was just too smart.

Without the moon, the desert night sky cloaked his actions. Opening the passenger door, he pulled the body from his vehicle and dragged the man out into the brush. It had been easy enough to slip something into Bryce's drink and watch him fall asleep. After he was unconscious, smothering him was a piece of cake.

The man had no class. And no brains if he thought he could blackmail him. Of course, Joyce thought he didn't have any brains. She'd taken that report and planned to expose him. He'd taken care of most of his loose ends. What he needed now was to find what Joyce had taken.

He left the body by a rock. The scavengers would take care of Bryce, and no one would be the wiser.

Too bad he couldn't let everyone know how he'd outsmarted them.

He shrugged. Oh, well, it was his little secret.

When Daniel walked into police headquarters and checked his box, he found a note from Jonathan Littledeer. Jon needed to talk to him.

Settling at his desk, he picked up the phone and dialed Jon in Albuquerque.

"Jon, what have you got for me?"

"We found the body of Felix Glasner. The body was discovered outside Santa Domingo Pueblo. It looks like he fell from the ruins built into the side of the mountain."

"Does anyone know what he was doing there?" Daniel asked.

"One of the guys in his office said Felix got a call about a rare Anasazi basket found in the pueblo. He was going to verify if it was a true Anasazi. He didn't come back."

It was too convenient. It certainly covered Preston Jones's backside. If the art expert bit the dust, then he couldn't say what was in the report they found in Elena's shop.

"The story smells," Daniel commented.

"That's my reading on it, too. Especially after that mess we found in his house. I don't believe in happy accidents."

One of the great things about Jon was he thought a lot like Daniel. When the two of them were in combat, they could guess each other's moves. More than once, Jon had covered Daniel and saved him.

"Thanks, Jon, for the info. I'm coming to your

fair city to talk to a couple of the folks at Real Deal."

"Do you want me to back you up?"

"Appreciate that."

"Also, I want to look at Felix's files."

"You want me to get the court order?"

"Yes. We want to cover all our bases."

"Then I'll see you in a couple of hours."

Daniel hung up the phone. This might be the lead that would crack this case.

Elena walked into the old adobe building on the north side of Albuquerque. She'd brought the Mendoza painting for evaluation. She also wanted to ask some questions about Felix Glasner's review of the painting she had the partial information on. The Real Deal Art Experts had remodeled an old department store on the north side of town. The adobe building had an air of timelessness set against the browns and reds of the surrounding desert.

Elena nodded at the receptionist. "I have an appointment to see Carrie Nash."

The young man dialed Carrie's number and told her that her appointment was here. "Go back," he instructed Elena.

She walked down the hall to the small corner office that Carrie shared with another appraiser.

"Elena, what have you brought me?"

Elena showed her the picture.

"Oh, if that's a real Mendoza you've found a big treasure. I'll call our expert and have a report for you by the end of the week."

"Thanks." Elena hesitated a moment, then pulled the partial report out of her purse. "Could you help me with this? I found it in an old spice chest in my store."

She handed the partial report to Carrie. The woman scanned it, then looked up. "Is this connected with Felix's disappearance?"

"I don't know. But it shouldn't have been in my store. I thought if I knew what the rest of the report said, it might help."

Carrie bit her lip, then nodded. "Okay. Let's look." She typed into the computer the reference number on top of the report. "We're lucky that all reports are kept in a central file, so anyone in the company can access them and review them."

The report appeared on the screen. Elena stood over Carrie and they read the analysis of the painting. The first line of the report stopped them. "Although a good copy, the painting is not the original."

"It's fake?" Elena breathed.

"It looks like it."

Elena stared at the screen. The copy was worth

maybe one hundred and fifty dollars. The original would be worth fifteen thousand.

"That's quite a difference," Carrie said.

"I wonder if Preston knew."

"It certainly would upset me," Carrie added.

"Would you make a copy of that for me?" Elena asked.

A knock on Carrie's door startled them. The door opened and Kevin Sanders, the president of Real Deal entered. Following him was Daniel Stillwater and another man.

"Carrie, this is Detective Stillwater from Santa Fe Police and Detective Littledeer from Albuquerque PD."

Elena didn't know what was going on but worried that maybe Daniel had followed her here.

"Detective Littledeer came to tell me that they found Felix's body in the Santo Domingo Pueblo. They want to talk to some of Felix's coworkers to see if they know anything about what he was working on."

Carrie's panic showed in her eyes. "Tuesday, Felix got a call. Someone wanted to sell Anasazi baskets they found. When I asked Felix about it, he wasn't forthcoming about where he was going. But he was very excited about the call."

"That was this Tuesday?" Jon Littledeer asked.

"Yes." Two days ago.

Elena met Daniel's gaze.

"The painting was a forgery, Daniel," Elena informed him.

"What's going on?" Kevin asked.

Elena had dealt with Kevin. He was a close friend of her mother's. She explained to him about finding the partial report in her shop and the break-ins to her store.

Carrie blushed. "Since we all have access to the reports, I didn't think it was a problem," she explained to her boss.

Both detectives stepped to the monitor and read the report.

"Why don't you print off a copy of the report for us," Jon ordered.

"Of course."

Report in hand, they moved to Felix's office and searched it. Among the files on Felix's computer, they found a report done for Cam McGinnis. He'd had several pieces of jewelry evaluated—several brooches done by Tiffany.

Her name was also listed in the computer. Real Deal authenticated several pieces of furniture for their store, the spice chest among them.

The detectives moved on to several other employees of the firm.

Her mind whirling, Elena walked out of the business. The news that the detectives delivered had shaken her. On unsteady legs, she moved to her car. Closing her eyes, she leaned against the fender of her car. "Oh, Lord, will this nightmare ever end?"

"Elena."

Daniel's voice seemed to be an answer to prayer. His hand settled on her back. She turned to face him.

"Another murder, yes?" she asked.

"We can't be sure. The body fell off a high cliff."

She laid her head on his chest. He wrapped his arms around her, resting his chin on her head.

"Death is never easy, Elena."

"There are too many around me, Daniel, that are dying." She looked up at him. "Why?"

"I wish I knew. But things are starting to come together. Jon will be working on it from this end."

She pulled back.

"I'll see you tonight?" he asked.

"I wouldn't disappoint April."

He leaned close and brushed his lips over hers. "I look forward to seeing you later."

How just the brush of his lips could make her heart race awed her. "Okay."

As she drove away, she realized that in the midst of this awful mess, the Lord had brought Daniel and April into her life.

April fidgeted as they drove to Rosalyn's house.

"You think she's coming?" April asked, a note of uncertainty in her voice.

"I think she will."

April nodded and looked out the window at the passing scenery.

Daniel felt fairly certain that Elena would not disappoint his daughter, but how well did he know the woman? He knew the statistics about her, height, weight, where she lived, but was she a person who kept her word? His gut told him she would, but gambling his daughter's happiness on it was another thing altogether.

When he turned the corner onto the street where Rosalyn lived, Elena's car was parked out front.

"She's here," April shrieked, bouncing up and down.

He parked behind Elena's car. Before he'd shut off the engine, April had her seat belt off and door open.

"C'mon, Dad."

He followed behind at a slower pace. When he walked in the front door, he saw April running into the kitchen at the far end of the house. He followed the voices through the living room and dining room.

"You brought a present?" April's voice rang with awe. When he reached the kitchen, April stood at the kitchen table holding a gaily wrapped small box in her hands.

"It's a birthday party, isn't it?" Elena replied. Her gaze met his and from the faint smile curving her lips, he guessed she found something amusing.

"What's so funny?"

"You're getting a little slow, Dad," Elena teased.

"I'm telling you, you don't know what a whirl-wind is until you have a daughter."

Elena bit her lips, trying to hide her smile.

He looked to Rosalyn for support, but she simply shook her head as if to say "men."

"Set the table, Daniel," Rosalyn ordered. "Use my nice dishes. And we're going to eat in the dining room."

Most meals were in the oversize kitchen. Rosalyn's house, built in the early 1900s, had a won-derful charm that always drew Daniel. But special-occasions meals were held in the dining room.

He walked into the other room and opened the china cabinet. Elena appeared at his side and held out her hands. "I'll do plates. You do silverware."

"Deal."

They worked in companionable silence. Being with this woman was a strange combination of excitement and comfort. She was the kind of woman whom a man could spend the rest of his life with.

"When I got back to the shop this afternoon, both Preston and Cam came over to the shop and mentioned Felix's death."

Daniel stilled. "How did they know about it? The information has not been released to the public or the news media."

"I don't know. But I didn't tell either one about you visiting Real Deal with Detective Littledeer."

"Good thinking."

The smell of refried beans and enchiladas filled the air.

Elena's stomach growled. "I'm ready to eat."

"Me, too," April announced.

Rosalyn put the pan on the table. Daniel helped with the bowl of refried beans and rice. Once all the food had made it to the table, they sat. Daniel prayed.

The meal went quickly with April informing everyone of her schoolwork and the stupid boy who kept bothering her.

"Maybe he likes you," Elena observed.

"Ick." April stuck out her tongue. "He's just so gross."

"That's true at your age," Elena agreed. "But you may feel differently in a couple of years."

Daniel paled.

She leaned over and whispered, "Don't worry, Dad. You've got probably another couple of years."

"That's what I'm afraid of."

"It's time for cake and presents," Rosalyn announced.

April jumped up and down. "Yes."

Daniel slipped out of the room and went to the hall closet where he'd hidden April's present. He brought the large present to the table.

"Wow," April breathed.

After a round of "Happy Birthday" and cake, April tore into the presents. Opening Daniel's, she saw an artist's tablet and watercolors. There were also several packages of chalk.

She looked up at her dad.

"You are a good artist. I want to give you the right materials for you to draw."

"Thank you, Daddy." She ran around the table and hugged him.

"There's also something else in that box."

Hurrying back to the present, she looked under the tablet. She held up the certificate, a frown creasing her brow.

"What does it say?" Elena asked.

"Art lessons with Jolie Torres?"

Elena gasped. Everyone looked at her.

"Who is she?" April asked.

"She's the hottest artist in the area. She does watercolors and is a renowned teacher. You are very fortunate to have her agree to teach you."

April's eyes grew large as she grasped the meaning of the gift, then ran to her father and gave him another hug. "Thank you, Daddy."

Daniel closed his eyes and felt his daughter's excitement.

April pulled back. "How did you know?"

Laughing, he cupped her face. "Because on every scrap of paper around the house I find your drawings. You are good, sweetheart. All you need is training."

His daughter's eyes glowed with anticipation.

"How did you get lessons with Jolie?" Elena wondered out loud. When she heard her own voice, she flushed.

"Jolie and I went to school together. She was also a friend of my wife. I took some of April's drawings to her, and she was impressed."

"Really, Dad. Did you show her my pictures?"

"I did." He nodded toward Elena's present. "You haven't opened the other present."

April ran back around the table and grabbed the gift from Elena. She tore open the wrapping and opened the box. Inside on cotton lining was a silver bracelet inlayed with turquoise. The open C shape was slipped on the wrist. April held it up for everyone to see. "It's beautiful!"

Daniel stared at Elena. He wanted to object, but he knew the gift was out of Elena's heart. "Are you sure?" he whispered.

"Yes." She beckoned April to her side. "I had one of these when I was your age. My mother gave it to me on my eighth birthday."

"Is this yours?" April asked.

"No. Mine is at the house, but when I looked at my bracelet, I thought of Mother. I remember her telling me that I was meant to wear silver and turquoise." Elena pulled the cross from under her blouse and showed it to April. "I still wear turquoise and silver. Wear your bracelet to honor your mother."

April's eyes filled with moisture. She slipped the bracelet onto her wrist. "Thank you." She hugged Elena.

Words failed Daniel. The woman constantly

amazed him. Her caring and thoughtfulness not only touched April's heart, but his, as well.

Love, his head whispered.

That was a truth he wasn't ready to hear.

TWELVE

"Anna Delao was bragging that their report would be the best, because her mother had a map of the New Mexico territory." April frowned. "And she wasn't nice at all." She imitated the girl.

Elena tried not to smile. She glanced at Daniel and saw the laughter dancing in his eyes.

Leaning forward on the couch, Elena said, "What if you had several pictures from before statehood?"

April's eyes widened. "Really? That would be just way cool."

"I have several pictures at the shop of Santa Fe in the 1880s. And a couple of pictures of people standing downtown."

"Really?"

"I do. Would you like to see them? Maybe even show them to your class?"

"You're kidding me."

"No. If you want to see them, we can go now."

She looked at her father. "Can we go?" Clasping her hands, she added, "Please?"

"I don't see why not."

"Yeah." She jumped up and danced around.

Outside, Daniel told Elena that he would follow her.

"Can I ride with Elena?" April asked.

"It's fine with me," Elena reassured Daniel.

"Okay, but don't talk her to death," Daniel warned his daughter.

"Sure, Daddy."

It only took ten minutes to get from Rosalyn's house to the shop. Daniel parked in front of the shop, while Elena and April parked in the alley and used the back door.

"Evening, Elena," Cam called out as he locked up his shop.

She introduced April to Cam. "You're working late tonight," Elena commented.

"I promised a customer she'd have this ring for tomorrow. I just finished."

They waved to him and entered Past Treasures. Elena hurried to the front door.

"What took you so long?" Daniel asked. "I was beginning to get worried."

"We ran into Cam in the alley. He'd had to finish an order."

Daniel frowned. Elena walked to the part of the shop where the pictures she spoke about were displayed.

"Wow," April breathed. She picked up the picture. Her bracelet slid down her arm and clanked against the frame. She took off the bracelet and set it on the table. "The city wasn't very big."

"Not compared to today," Elena replied. She moved to the next row and picked up a second picture. City Hall, 1900. April took the picture reverently and gazed at the buildings. She glanced up, wonder in her eyes. "This is so much better than what Anna had."

Daniel looked at the old frames and curved glass. "Are you sure you want to lend those? They look expensive."

Smiling, Elena answered, "I'm sure I want April to beat Anna." Elena touched the first picture. "That is of Santa Fe in 1885 in the spring."

Daniel's cell phone rang. "Stillwater here."

Elena and April watched as Daniel's expression darkened. "Where was he found?" He listened and nodded. "Okay, I'll be there ASAP." He closed the cell phone and looked at his daughter. "We have to go."

April's shoulders sagged. She didn't complain, but her disappointment showed in her eyes.

Elena couldn't take it. "Daniel, would it help if I took April back to Rosalyn's home?"

He hesitated. "Yes. I shouldn't be long, but if something happens, then she'll be at Rosalyn's and can go to sleep."

"I'll be happy to drive her."

"Okay. You lock up behind me and I'll wait until I see you drive away."

Elena locked the door after Daniel and she and April hurried out the back door of the store with the two pictures. They waved to Daniel as they exited the alley and started off in the opposite direction.

Daniel drove toward the stretch of desert northwest of Santa Fe where the body of Bryce Green was discovered. The CSI guys would wait for him and Raul to observe the scene before they processed it.

His phone rang again. Raul. He described the scene. "Hikers had found the body behind a large boulder. He'd been stabbed."

"Was there any attempt to hide the body?"

"Minimal. And this isn't the primary scene."

Bryce had been murdered elsewhere.

"It seems that all the people connected with his case are being knocked off," Raul commented.

"Our killer is trying to cover his tracks. But he's not been successful. He keeps leaving bodies, and we keep finding them."

"How long before you're here?"

"Give me ten minutes." Daniel closed his phone. Was it an accident that the cops kept running into these bodies, or was their killer trying to throw him off?

"Oh, Elena, I left my bracelet at your shop," April exclaimed, a stricken look on her face.

"That's okay, April. I'll get it tomorrow."

"But I want to show it to all my friends. Could we go back and get it?"

April's eyes held such disappointment that Elena didn't have the heart to deny her. "Okay. Let's go get it."

They turned around and drove back to the shop. Elena parked in the front and pulled out her keys. Once the door was opened, she disarmed the alarm.

"Do you remember where you put it?"

"It's on the table where we got the pictures," April replied, running to the table. Grabbing the bracelet, she turned and a hand came out grasping April's arm. She screamed.

"Shut up," the figure demanded. She couldn't see the man's face, but the voice was familiar.

"Let me go," April screamed. The man tried to jerk April close, but she turned and bit him on the arm. The man released her.

April raced to Elena's side, and they retreated behind the glass display case at the front of the store. April shook like a young tree in a strong wind. Elena wrapped her arm around April and drew her close.

"What are we going to do?" April whispered.

Although panic beat at her heart and brain, Elena tried to remain calm. *Lord, show me the way,* she silently prayed.

"I need those documents that Joyce stole, Elena."

Preston.

"I don't know what you're talking about, Preston," Elena answered.

"I don't believe you." He slowly approached.

Elena looked around for a way of escape. In the light from the streetlights, Elena could see a gun in Preston's hand. No matter what, she would *not* allow another person she loved to be murdered. She'd been a child before, but now she could do something.

Squatting, she placed her mouth next to April's ear. "I'm going to distract him. You race toward the front door and don't you stop for any reason, do you understand?"

April nodded.

"Once you're out of here, run. Get to safety, then call the police."

Fright showed in the little girl's eyes, but she nodded her head. "Okay."

Elena looked around for something to distract Preston. On the top of the case was a glass paperweight with an old Spanish coin inside. Turning, she asked, "Are you ready?"

"Yes."

"Count to three."

April held up one finger. Two fingers. And when the third finger went up, both of them stood, Elena scooped up the paperweight and pitched it at Preston. He ducked.

April raced around the counter and headed for the door.

Elena picked up another item, a jade bird, and hurled it at Preston. She hit her mark, and the gun went off. April squealed.

"Go," Elena shouted.

April didn't stop, but ran out the door.

Not wanting Preston to move toward April, Elena picked up another object, a brass apple, and threw it.

This time she failed to hit Preston. Instead, he fired his gun at her. The glass case shattered. Several pieces of glass hit Elena.

Pain burned in her upper arm and she felt the blood trickle down her right cheek. But it didn't matter. She would fight Preston no matter what happened.

With each mile Daniel drove, the tension in his neck grew. Something was wrong. But what? What?

His mind raced over all the disjointed details of this case, but nothing jelled.

Opening his phone, he called Elena's cell. She didn't answer. With each ring, his muscles tightened. After the seventh ring, it went to voice mail.

He knew without a doubt something was wrong. Quickly, he dialed Rosalyn. When she picked up, he asked, "Are Elena and April there?"

"No. Aren't they with you?"

His heart stopped. He fought the panic. He couldn't help Elena or April if he let fear overwhelm him. "If you hear from them, Rosalyn, call my cell." He disconnected and dialed Raul. "I'm not coming. Something's wrong. I can't get hold of Elena and April. I'm going back to find them."

"Do you want me to call backup for your location?"

"Do that. Have them go to Elena's shop."

As he sped back to Past Treasures, he prayed with an intensity he never experienced before. "Lord, keep them safe."

Elena hid behind the antique wardrobe. Blood trickled down her neck and her arm throbbed.

"Where is it, Elena?" His desperate voice rushed out of the dark.

"I don't know, Preston. I only found part of the report. The first page."

"I don't believe you," he answered, coming closer.

Elena looked around for a way to get to either door. Preston stood in between her and the front door. And to get to the back door, she'd have to run a gauntlet of furniture, then unlock it. And most of the way, she'd be an easy target.

"Daniel and I found the first page together. He's seen it and the police in Albuquerque have seen it, too. We've been to Real Deal and talked to them about the report. We know about the fake painting, Preston."

"You didn't talk to Felix, Elena. I know."

She grew cold. "Why is that?"

"He was elsewhere."

Elena knew this forgery hadn't been an isolated incident. "How long have you and Felix been working with each other?"

"Long enough. Felix suddenly decided he had a conscience. He wasn't going to cooperate with me anymore." His laugh, laced with bitterness, surrounded her, making her skin crawl. "Like his hands were clean."

Something crashed.

She darted to a large carved Spanish chair, trying to hide behind it. *Help, Lord.*

"Joyce had nothing to do with your business. Why kill her?"

"I thought the woman wanted—we went out. When we came back to my shop, she—led me on, then she ripped off that report," he ground out. "She thought I didn't know that she had it, but I figured it out. When I demanded it back, she told me that I needed to tell the client about the fake and return the money I got. I told her to mind her own business. I wasn't the one who went to prison for passing funny money."

Elena knew that if he'd thrown that in Joyce's face, it had probably sealed his fate. She'd planned on turning him in. "Preston, if you leave now, maybe you can disappear before the cops catch up to you. You could start over somewhere else." She crab-walked to the old dining table surrounded by four chairs.

"But I'm sure you'll fill the cops in."

"Preston, I have no control over the cops. You can start again. You know a lot about art. You have a good eye."

He didn't respond.

She looked around for any weapon or something she could use to distract him. She saw a Tiffany floor lamp. If she could send that crashing, she could distract him. The lamp was worth a lot of money, but she didn't think anyone would complain. With her mind made up, she crawled across the floor to the lamp.

"You're not going to get out of here, Elena, so just quit playing."

She ignored him and grabbed the base of the lamp and shoved it. It fell on his arm, causing his gun to go off.

Daniel sped around the final corner to see the square on which Elena's shop was located. Someone darted out.

"Dad."

Daniel slammed on his brakes, threw the car into Park and opened his door. April raced into his arms.

"What's wrong, sweetheart?"

She looked up at him. "I left my bracelet in the shop. I begged her to go back. There was a man. He had a gun. Elena helped me to get out." Tears ran down April's face. "I'm so sorry."

He cupped her face in his hands. "It's okay. I want you to get into the backseat and huddle down on the floorboard. Do not get out of the car until I come and get you. Do you understand?"

She nodded.

As she scrambled into the backseat, Daniel notified dispatch where he was and what had happened.

He parked on the other side of Preston's store and pulled out his phone, handing it to April. "Call Raul and tell him what happened."

"Okay." She gulped. "Please be careful, Papa."

"Pray, sweetie."

He got out of the car and softly closed the door. As he approached the door to Elena's shop, he heard the crash. Instinct took over and he raced to the front door and peered inside. He opened the door and slipped inside. It took a moment for his eyes to adjust to the darkness. He saw a movement in the middle of the room.

He moved that direction. "Give it up," he called out. "There are several patrol cars on the way."

"Daniel," Elena called out. "Be careful. Preston is out of his mind. He thinks if he kills us all, that will make everything better."

"Shut up," Preston shouted.

"We found the body, Preston," Daniel called out.

"What body?" he yelled back.

Daniel moved into the room. "Hikers found the body of Bryce. My partner is out there at Santo Domingo Pueblo."

Silence greeted his answer. He struggled to see into the blackness.

The sound of breaking glass broke the silence.

Panic raced up Daniel's spine. "Elena."

"If you want to see Ms. Jackson live," Preston shouted, "you'll back off and let us leave."

Daniel strained to see. Sirens filled the air and lights from the arriving cruisers flooded through the front windows. He saw Preston's arm locked around Elena's neck.

"Now, after you put down your weapon, you're going to tell the men outside to step aside and let us leave, or she dies."

Daniel's worst nightmare had come to life. He put his gun on the floor. "You'll not get far," Daniel warned.

Preston simply smiled and put the muzzle of his gun to Elena's temple.

"Okay." Daniel backed toward the front door. Opening it, he yelled, "There's a hostage situation here. He's demanding a car and safe passage."

Daniel looked at the team of officers gathered outside. Raul's car pulled up to the shop and he slipped out of the car. Daniel's eyes met Raul's, and Daniel prayed that his partner would read his silent message not to allow Preston to leave.

Daniel turned back to Preston. He'd moved toward the door.

"You can use my partner's car."

"No," Preston shot back. "We'll use Elena's." He jerked Elena's neck. "You got your keys?"

"They're in my pocket."

Preston pushed her to the door. Daniel backed out onto the sidewalk.

"Keep backing up," Preston instructed.

Daniel stepped into the street.

Preston pushed Elena toward her car.

"No," April shouted, darting out from between the parked cars. "Stop him, Dad."

Preston's gun moved to April.

"Run," Elena shouted, slamming the heel of her foot down on Preston's instep. His gun went off.

Daniel lunged toward Preston, but before he could reach Elena, she drove her elbow into

Preston's belly, then whirled, and with an upward motion, brought the heel of her hand under Preston's chin. He staggered back and fell through the front window of Past Treasures.

April tried to move forward, but was caught by one of the patrolmen.

Daniel and Raul pulled a bleeding Preston out of the window and cuffed him.

"Go see to your April," Raul instructed Daniel.

The patrolman let April go, and she ran into her father's arms. Daniel scooped her up and wrapped his arms around his precious daughter. Burying his face into her neck, he breathed a prayer of thanks. Turning to thank Elena, he saw the blood on her face and throat.

"You're bleeding."

Elena wiped away the blood. "It's nothing. I got cut by flying glass."

April rested her head on Daniel's shoulder. "She saved me, Dad. I was so scared, but she threw a glass ball at that man and hit him. I ran out the door." She wiggled in his embrace. He placed her on her feet. She moved to Elena's side and wrapped her arms around her waist and rested her head on her chest. Elena's startled expression flew to Daniel's.

"I was afraid he'd hurt you," April whispered, her voice thick. She looked up. "And he did."

"I'm okay." Elena stroked April's head. "I couldn't let him hurt you, April. But we work well as a team."

April raised her head. "I'm sorry I asked you to come back. It's my fault."

Elena knelt before April and wiped the tears from her cheeks. "In your wildest dreams, you never would've put me or yourself in danger. You know how much your father loves you and how it would hurt him."

April looked down. With a finger, Elena raised the little girl's chin. "It's not your fault. Preston was doing very bad things, and we got caught in them. But you and your father saved us." She looked up at him.

Swallowing hard, he nodded at Elena.

Raul appeared by April's side.

"Are you okay?" he demanded.

She nodded and hugged him.

Tears glistened in his eyes. "I'm so glad you're all right, sweetheart."

"You helped," she whispered.

He released her and turned to Daniel. Running his hands through his hair, he whispered, "I nearly lost it when she called me. The guys at the other crime scene gave me some strange looks."

Patting his partner on the back, Daniel said, "If anyone gives you any lip, I'll take care of it."

April tugged at Raul's shirt. When he looked down she whispered, "I won't tell anyone the bad words you said."

Raul's startled gaze met Daniel's. Daniel fought the smile.

"Thanks," Raul whispered to April.

She patted his hand.

With the crime-scene crew there, the detectives were forced out of the shop. They returned to police headquarters, where Daniel, April and Elena were each debriefed about what happened at Past Treasures.

Raul talked to Elena, questioning her on the sequence of events. When her statement was typed up and she'd signed it and handed back the pen, Raul said, "You've made a difference in his life."

Her brows furrowed. "What are you talking about?"

Leaning back, he crossed his arms over his chest. "Daniel. The man broke into a smile yesterday for no reason at all. And he's done other suspicious things. I caught him whistling."

Elena stared at Raul. "I don't understand. We all smile and whistle."

"No. Daniel, when he was assigned to be my

partner, had just buried Nita. A more closed-up man I've never seen. He always did his work, but something was riding him hard." He drummed his fingers on the file on the desk. "Since he walked into the office at your store, the man's been different."

Raul's words surprised her.

"I've also seen a difference in April. That little girl's heart broke when her mother died. Daniel has done his best to help her. But when she looked at you tonight, I saw a spark that hasn't been there for a long time."

"It was only the excitement of the night," Elena offered. The excuse sounded lame even to her own ears.

"I'm a cop, lady. I know a lie when I hear it."

"Why are you telling me this?" she bit out.

"Because you need to stop fighting whatever it is that's chewing at you and go with the flow."

He stood, took the file and left the room.

It was too much to think about. Grabbing her purse, she left the room. In the hall, she ran into Daniel. He carried April, who was asleep, her head resting on his shoulder.

They stared at each other.

"Thank you," he whispered.

She nodded and walked by him.

* * *

Daniel tucked April into her bed. "I was scared, but I knew that Elena wouldn't let him hurt me."

He sat beside her on the bed. "I'm glad both of you were okay, but you shouldn't have gone back to the shop."

Squirming under his rebuke, she mumbled, "That was my fault."

"Did you learn from what happened?" he asked.

"I did. And I promise I'll follow what you say to me."

He smiled and kissed her forehead, wondering if he could use that promise when she was sixteen. "I love you, sunshine."

"I love you, too, Daddy."

As he started to close her bedroom door, she said, "I hope you're not mad at Elena. She saved us."

"I'm not."

Leaving her, he sought refuge in his room. His mind went over tonight's incident, and what he knew was his child had been restored to him. But he also had to admit that if something had happened to Elena, his heart would've been crushed.

He was in love. His shoulders slumped and his head hung down. Love.

And Elena seemed to love April. His daughter certainly returned the feelings. The question was did Elena love April's papa?

"Lord, I messed up so much with Nita. I don't know if I can be successful this time, but I pray you would show me the way."

He opened his Bible and searched for the love chapter. He read I Corinthians 13. When he got to verse 7 the words rang in his heart. *Love always protects, always trusts, always hopes, always perseveres.*

They were actions. Not feelings. And Elena protected his daughter tonight.

The verse didn't say that love was always perfect. He certainly knew he wasn't perfect. But he could try.

Closing his eyes, a sense of peace settled over him. He knew what he had to do.

Daniel waited for April to show up at the table for breakfast. She bounced in, singing and smiling, apparently no worse for her adventure last night.

"Hi, Dad." She kissed him, then nabbed an apricot empanada and began to eat.

On the table lay the newspaper. The front-page story was about Preston Jones and how he'd tried to take April and Elena hostage.

"Wow," she muttered around her empanada.

Daniel went to the refrigerator and poured a glass of milk and gave it to her.

He sat across from her. "There'll be talk today. Questions from your friends. If you want to stay with Rosalyn today, that will be fine."

"Why? I'll be a celebrity."

In spite of her bravado, Daniel knew that April would need to talk about what happened. He wouldn't push the issue today.

"Okay. School it is." He looked down at the table, trying to find the right words. "I'm going to see Elena today, April. I'm going to ask her to marry me. I wondered if—"

She leaped out of her chair and threw her arms around his neck. "I'm so glad. Sooooo glad."

"Then I guess you don't have a problem with that?"

"Pleease, Dad. I knew at the church carnival that you two should marry. I just wondered when you two would know."

"Really?"

She gave him a look that said, she was the expert, and why did he doubt her? "Really."

"Then wish me good luck."

"Better, Dad. I've been praying."

Out of the mouths of babes.

* * *

Elena knew she couldn't go back to the shop this morning. Diane understood that. She'd gone into the shop and told Elena not to worry about anything but resting and listening to her heart. God had answers for her.

That piece of advice stumped Elena. And as for her heart, it was mute.

The doorbell chimed. She didn't want to face anyone right now. She refused to answer it. Instead she stared into her coffee mug.

The bell rang again. She resisted the urge to answer it. Maybe whoever it was would go away.

With a final chug of her coffee, she got up and headed for the sink, pausing to look out at the mountains in the distance. Daniel appeared at the back door. He tried the handle and it opened. "Why didn't you answer the door?"

"How did you know I was here?"

"Because I talked to your mother." He stepped close. "Why didn't you answer the door?"

"Because I didn't want to talk to anyone."

"I've been talking with everyone. Albuquerque PD, the people at Real Deal, the State Police since that's where Preston dumped Bryce's body outside the Santo Domingo Pueblo."

She turned her back to him and set her coffee mug in the sink.

He leaned back against the counter next to her. "It seems Preston had a lucrative business. He would come across valuable paintings, then with the aid of Felix, who had contacts, would make a copy of the painting. Then Felix would certify the forgery and they would sell both the original and forgery. The forgery with the 'funny paperwork' would sell for the same price." He folded his arms over his chest. "It's going to be sticky to tell all those people and art galleries they have forgeries."

She turned and leaned back against the counter. "I can imagine the hit Real Deal is going to take. I'm sure the owners would like nothing more than to kill Felix again."

"It was Bryce's body discovered last night. I can only guess that Bryce discovered Preston had killed his ex-wife and tried to blackmail him."

"What a mess."

"How are you doing?" he quietly asked.

"I'm okay." Her cheek occasionally throbbed from where the bullet grazed her, but other than that, she was fine, physically.

"I'm sorry I put April in that position. I never should've gone back to the shop with the trouble we've been having."

His fingers skated over her cheek. Her gaze met his and found tenderness there. She'd been expecting rebuke or anger, but not the gentle concern she saw there.

"You need to take the advice you gave to April. Don't blame yourself for Preston's actions."

Her gaze slid from his. "I screwed up."

"I think maybe your blaming yourself is the easy way out."

Jerking back, she said, "What are you talking about?"

"Guilt. I forgive you. April forgives you. She blames herself. We all make mistakes. God forgives us.

"But when you found yourself cornered by Preston, you fought back and saved April. Are you sure your guilt is from last night. Or is it from the day your mother died."

His words hit the target. She didn't realize the feelings she grappled with were mixed up with the emotions from so long ago.

"It's true, Elena. You put yourself between danger and my daughter. I admire you. And I love you."

He pulled her into his arms and brushed his lips over hers. He rested his forehead on hers.

"You are an amazing woman, Elena. From the

instant I laid eyes on you, my heart came to life. And my daughter's smile has returned. Somehow, someway, you've given her smile back to her. Thank you."

"You're welcome." His hand ran over her hair, then tilted her head so he could gently kiss her. "Last night, something inside me told me to go back to your shop. I knew in those desperate minutes that I not only loved my April, but I loved the woman with her.

"Since the moment we met, you've touched my heart. I didn't want to love again, because I was so lousy the last time with my wife. But my heart didn't listen. I love you, Elena. And I want to marry you."

Her mind reeled. This man, who'd touched her heart in ways she couldn't count, loved her. "What does April think?"

"She was ready for me to propose days ago."

She could imagine what the irrepressible child said. "Well, as long as I have her approval, then yes, I'll marry you."

They kissed and she rested her head on his chest again. She thought she heard him say, "Thank you, Lord."

EPILOGUE

Christmas trees lined the reception hall of First Community Church. Since Elena and Daniel decided to get married the first of December, they used the season's colors. April, dressed in a green velvet gown, danced with her dad. She beamed. Daniel looked dashing in his tux. The sight of him and April brought such joy to Elena's heart that she wanted to pinch herself.

"Thank you, Lord," she whispered. Out of grief and tragedy, He brought joy into her life. Each day that had passed, Elena had marveled how her family had adopted Daniel and April. April thrived on Diane's spoiling. Between Diane and Rosalyn, April would never lack for anything, emotionally or physically.

Diane was on the dance floor, too, dancing in the arms of her adopted brother, Adrian. He'd flown in from Seattle with his family for the wedding.

Cam stopped by her side. "I think your new husband is a keeper."

She glanced at him. "You don't hold a grudge against him for his suspicions of you?"

"Not after we discovered who was the real bad guy." He shook his head. "Who would've thought?"

"Well, look at it this way, Cam. You now have friends on the police force."

"I guess."

A noise at the door of the reception hall drew Elena's attention. A tall man dressed in an air force dress uniform appeared. He scanned the room until he got to her. The instant their eyes met, she knew who he was.

Her hand flew to her mouth. "Rafe," she whispered.

The music died and the room fell silent, but she had eyes for no one else. Slowly, she started toward him. His long legs ate up the distance and he scooped her up into his arms.

"Sis," he breathed.

Tears flowed.

"What's going on, Dad?"

Elena heard April's voice. She whispered into

Rafe's ear, "You better let me go or my new cop husband might get the wrong idea."

He laughed and set her back on her feet. She grabbed Rafe's hand and turned to face her husband. Behind Daniel stood Raul, Adrian, and Diane. April stood in front of her father. They were all ready for battle.

"Daniel, April, Mom, I want you to meet my brother Rafael Segura."

A stunned silence held the crowd for a moment, then Daniel stepped forward and offered his hand.

That broke the ice and Elena individually introduced each person to Rafe.

After several minutes of introductions, Rafe sat down with Elena's new family and explained that about six months ago, he hired a private detective to find Elena.

"That's who the guy was taking pictures," Daniel said. "You are going to stay with us awhile?"

"I've got time off through the New Year."

Elena hugged Rafe's arm. "Good."

Later that night as Elena and Daniel stood in the honeymoon suite of their hotel in Taos, looking out to the mountains, Daniel whispered, "Are you happy?"

She turned in his arms and gently kissed him. "There are no words to describe it."

"I didn't know who that tall air force officer was when he walked in."

"I knew him instantly. My heart told me who he was. It was kind of like when I met you. I knew something was there."

"Oh?"

She laughed. "Now that I think about it, yeah."

He gave her a smug smile.

"This day has been a day, Daniel Stillwater, to give thanks. Not only has God restored my brother, He's given me a family that was beyond my wildest dreams."

"Amen," he whispered.

"Amen," she echoed.

Dear Reader,

When I was a small child, my mother took me to New Mexico (Santa Fe, Albuquerque and Las Vegas) to visit family. I fell in love with the scenery and the rich Spanish background of the state. And the food—I adore it. Refried beans cooked with lard are the best. Those memories of New Mexico inspired this story. For Elena, her childhood was a nightmare, but God can make beauty out of ashes and He can heal the pains of our past.

I've been writing all my adult life, and love a good mystery. I am no fun for my family when we go to movies with a mystery in them because I always poke holes in the plot or complain that the cops wouldn't act that way. My writing has also brought me into contact with many wonderful law-enforcement people—men and women. They have enriched my life.

The wonderful thing about writing is some-times we stumble upon the truth. As I wrote Elena's story, her compassion for April and tender heart were revelations to me. I hope you enjoy Daniel's, Elena's and April's journeys from wounded and hurting individuals to ones who have found peace and wholeness.

Sincerely,

Leann Harris

QUESTIONS FOR DISCUSSION

1. The murder of the shop employee throws Elena back into the terror of her childhood. Have you had such an experience? How has God helped you deal with that issue?

2. Elena's adoptive father was compassionate with her, yet didn't let her misbehave. He was very mindful of the trauma in her life. How did he model God's mercy and discipline for His children? How do you discipline your children? Has God disciplined you?

3. When Elena discovers Joyce's criminal record, what does she discover about her adoptive father's compassion?

4. Why does Daniel blame himself for his wife's cancer? Is that reasonable? Do you ever blame yourself for things you can't control? What can you do to deal with that guilt?

5. When Joyce's brother is informed of her death, he tells the detectives he isn't interested. She

committed a crime and he had no use for her. What do you think of his attitude? Have you run across people like that? How do you deal with them?

6. How does Elena minister to April at the restaurant and at the church fair? Why do you think she's doing it?

7. At the church fair, what does Elena discover about Daniel and the kind of man he is?

8. Daniel is caught off guard when his daughter invites Elena to her birthday party. How does he handle it? How do you handle unexpected surprises from your children?

9. What is Elena's birthday gift to April? How does it affect April? Daniel? Elena?

10. How is Daniel freed from his guilt about his wife's death? What truth does he speak to Elena and how does it affect him?

11. How does Daniel convince Elena to marry him? How is Elena's love put into action? Is

love a feeling? Or is it action? What is your definition of love?

12. How is Elena's life restored at the end of the book? How has God restored things in your life?

Love Inspired
HISTORICAL
INSPIRATIONAL HISTORICAL ROMANCE

Adelaide Crum longs for a family, but the closed-minded town elders refuse to entrust even the most desperate orphan to a woman alone. Newspaperman Charles Graves promises to stand by her, despite his embittered heart. Adelaide's gentle soul soon makes him wonder if he can overcome his bitter past, and somehow find the courage to love....

Look for

Courting Miss Adelaide
by
JANET DEAN

Available September wherever books are sold, including most bookstores, supermarkets, drugstores and discount stores.

www.SteepleHill.com

Steeple
Hill®

LIH82796

Love Inspired

Only one person knows why Kat Thatcher left her Oklahoma hometown ten years ago. That person is Seth Washington. And now that she's back, he's only too available to talk about the past. Seth insists the Lord is on their side and always was. But will that be enough for love?

Look for

A Time To Heal

by

Linda Goodnight

Available September wherever books are sold, including most bookstores, supermarkets, drugstores and discount stores.

www.SteepleHill.com

Steeple Hill®

LI87497

REQUEST YOUR FREE BOOKS!
2 FREE RIVETING INSPIRATIONAL NOVELS
PLUS 2 FREE MYSTERY GIFTS

YES! Please send me 2 FREE Love Inspired® Suspense novels and my 2 FREE mystery gifts (gifts are worth about $10). After receiving them, if I don't wish to receive any more books, I can return the shipping statement marked "cancel". If I don't cancel, I will receive 4 brand-new novels every month and be billed just $4.24 per book in the U.S. or $4.74 per book in Canada, plus 25¢ shipping and handling per book and applicable taxes, if any*. That's a savings of over 20% off the cover price! I understand that accepting the 2 free books and gifts places me under no obligation to buy anything. I can always return a shipment and cancel at any time. Even if I never buy another book, the two free books and gifts are mine to keep forever.

123 IDN ERXX 323 IDN ERXM

Name	(PLEASE PRINT)
Address	Apt. #
City	State/Prov.	Zip/Postal Code

Signature (if under 18, a parent or guardian must sign)

Order online at www.LoveInspiredSuspense.com
Or mail to Steeple Hill Reader Service:

IN U.S.A.: P.O. Box 1867, Buffalo, NY 14240-1867
IN CANADA: P.O. Box 609, Fort Erie, Ontario L2A 5X3

Not valid to current subscribers of Love Inspired Suspense books.

Want to try two free books from another series?
Call 1-800-873-8635 or visit www.morefreebooks.com

* Terms and prices subject to change without notice. N.Y. residents add applicable sales tax. Canadian residents will be charged applicable provincial taxes and GST. Offer not valid in Quebec. This offer is limited to one order per household. All orders subject to approval. Credit or debit balances in a customer's account(s) may be offset by any other outstanding balance owed by or to the customer. Please allow 4 to 6 weeks for delivery. Offer available while quantities last.

Your Privacy: Steeple Hill Books is committed to protecting your privacy. Our Privacy Policy is available online at www.SteepleHill.com or upon request from the Reader Service. From time to time we make our lists of customers available to reputable third parties who may have a product or service of interest to you. If you would prefer we not share your name and address, please check here. ☐

LISUS08R

Inside ROMANCE

Stay up-to-date on all your romance reading news!

The Inside Romance newsletter is a FREE quarterly newsletter highlighting our upcoming series releases and promotions!

Click on the <u>Inside Romance</u> link on the front page of **www.eHarlequin.com** or e-mail us at insideromance@harlequin.ca to sign up to receive your FREE newsletter today!

You can also subscribe by writing us at: HARLEQUIN BOOKS
Attention: Customer Service Department
P.O. Box 9057, Buffalo, NY 14269-9057

Please allow 4-6 weeks for delivery of the first issue by mail.

Love Inspired®
SUSPENSE

TITLES AVAILABLE NEXT MONTH

Don't miss these four stories in September

DOUBLE CROSS by Terri Reed
The McClains
Her family's orchid farm is Kiki Brill's pride and joy. She
won't sell, no matter how much Ryan McClain offers. But as
accidents threaten her peaceful life on Maui, the wealthy,
handsome businessman, once the prime suspect, begins to
seem like her last hope.

BADGE OF HONOR by Carol Steward
In the Line of Fire
Why would FBI agent Sarah Roberts start over as a small-
town cop? She *has* to be undercover. And police officer
Nick Matthews knows exactly who Sarah is spying on: him.
Then Sarah's past crashes down on them. Trusting his new
partner becomes a matter of life, death—and love.

THE FACE OF DECEIT by Ramona Richards
Karen O'Neill barely remembers her parents' murder. Still,
she's haunted by a face—which she sculpts into her vases.
Now, an art buyer is dead and Karen's vases are being
shattered. Art expert Mason DuBroc believes the clues are
in the clay. Can they decode them in time?

FINAL DEPOSIT by Lisa Harris
It's bad enough that Lindsey Taylor's father lost his savings
in an Internet scam. Now he's gone to claim his "fortune,"
and Lindsey fears she'll never see him again. Financial
security expert Kyle Walker promises to help her. But the
closer they get, the more danger they find....

LISCNM0808